A HUGH RENNERT MYSTERY

# THE CAT SCREAMS

By
TODD DOWNING

**WILDSIDE PRESS**

www.wildsidepress.com

---

## FROM THE REVIEWS

"Mr. Downing seems to know his Mexico and has written a very good story about it, which turns out very unexpectedly and offers credible reasons for all the things that happen, including the cat's screams. . . ."

—*Chicago Tribune*

"The Mexican setting adds to the mystery and glamour of this story. . . ."

—*New York Times*

"It is a well-written and convincing story. The author deserves a laurel wreath for managing so cleverly elements which seemed to have no rational bearing on each other. . . ."

—*Boston Transcript*

---

# PROLOGUE: SUICIDE

(Translation from the Mexico City *Mundial*, of June 18, 193-)

## STRANGE EPIDEMIC OF SUICIDES
## PUZZLES AUTHORITIES

*Two More Die By Own Hands in Taxco Colony*

### FOREIGNERS IN PANIC

*Revival of Primitive Practices
Reported as United States
Citizens Are Found Dead*

TAXCO, June 18 (Special)—Is some malignant influence at work among the members of Taxco's brilliant foreign colony?

This is the question that is being asked as the picturesque little town which has become known in recent years as the rendezvous of artists and intellectuals suddenly finds its age-old peace threatened by the increasing prevalence of suicides and queer deaths.

Strange circumstances yesterday surrounded the deaths of two citizens of the United States. Last night two more visitors from the Northern republic committed suicide, for no apparent reason.

The body of Miss Helen Carstairs, about forty-five years old, thought to be a poet of the United States, was found early this morning upon the rocks below a balcony of the Hotel Borda, where she was staying. Her skull was fractured by the fall. Her death at first was attributed to an accident, until it was pointed

3

out that the height of the railing about the balcony precluded any such danger.

## Others Found Dead

A little later the same morning the body of Mrs. Irene Osterlow, elderly United States citizen, was found in her room at the Hotel Taxqueña. She was seated in a chair by a window facing the east. Both wrists had been slashed with a keen-bladed knife, and blood from the opened veins formed a shallow pool about her chair. Mrs. Osterlow was said to be extremely wealthy and has been wintering in Taxco.

The authorities refused to comment upon these deaths or upon the reported discovery of the body of a soldier upon one of the streets of Taxco during the previous night. Of the other deaths they said that they were "mere coincidences."

Various explanations were given by members of the foreign colony. Most held the opinion that it was, as the authorities claimed, coincidence, or that the series of suicides is due to the power of suggestion upon susceptible minds. It was pointed out that the young American who died yesterday in a popular pension of Taxco undoubtedly committed suicide.

## Alienist Not Alarmed

Meanwhile, queer rumors were current about the plaza. That native witch doctors still ply their trade among the ignorant persons of Taxco is a well-established fact, and one of these, a woman famous in her trade, is being sought by police. These *curanderas,* the ignorant ones believe, can injure or drive insane any person, provided they possess an article of his clothing.

Another curious circumstance is the unprecedented delay of the rains, which in the region of Taxco are usually in force at this time of year. That the long-continued dry season has begun to breed disease which preys upon the minds of unacclimated persons is a theory seriously advanced by many.

A scientist from the Capital, when asked for an opinion, scoffed at what he terms "superstitious fears" and pointed out parallels of simultaneous waves of suicides in scattered places throughout the world.

4

# CHAPTER ONE

### HARLEQUINADE

The young man sat upon the observation car of the Sunshine Special and stared into the blue mountains that sprawled upon the horizon.

The train had climbed high upon the Mexican plateau, and in never-ending rows the *magueyes* lifted sharp green claws from the gray-brown soil.

From time to time the young man would run his fingers nervously through his curly brick-red hair. After he had done this he would draw a flat bottle from his pocket and drink, with long gulps. He smoked one cigarette after another. He had been following this procedure, the pleasant-faced, somewhat elderly man who sat on the other side had noticed, for most of the day. He wasn't curious, this man, yet in the course of a two-day train trip one gets to notice rather closely the actions of one's fellow passengers.

The young man was stockily built, evidently still in his twenties. His head and face inclined to squareness, and his features were handsome in a rough-cut pugnacious fashion. His nose was slightly crooked, as if it had been broken at one time. The strength of his face was sapped by a weak mouth, oddly at variance with the rest of his features. He wore a well tailored brown tweed suit, badly in need of pressing.

It was a time-table which started the conversation. The elderly man had consulted it and was about to return it to his pocket when the young one said abruptly: "Mind if I look at that?"

"Certainly not," the other said pleasantly and handed it to him.

The young man turned the pages aimlessly for several minutes, then returned the booklet.

"Do you know anything about Mexico?" he asked.

"A little."

"How does one get to Taxco? It's down in the mountains south of Mexico City."

The other glanced at him with some interest.

"Buses run there from Cuernavaca," he said. "You can get to Cuernavaca from Mexico City by train or by bus."

Silence lay between them for a few minutes. The young man's gaze was on the rails and the clouds of gray dust that whipped them.

"You've been there?" he asked.

"Yes." The other paused and added: "I'm bound there now, as a matter of fact."

His companion paused in the act of lighting a cigarette.

"You are?" He finished the operation and tossed the match to the floor. "Maybe we'd better get acquainted, then. My name's Riddle. From Tulsa, Oklahoma."

"Mine is Rennert."

Riddle emitted a thin cloud of smoke from his nostrils and stared for a moment at the tip of his cigarette.

"What kind of a place is Taxco?" he asked.

Rennert smiled. He had been asked the question before.

"That depends on what you mean. It is quiet, restful, and beautiful. Those three adjectives, I believe, describe it. An old Spanish colonial town hidden away in the mountains. It has become quite a rendezvous for writers and artists from Mexico City and the United States."

"So I understand." Something that might have been bitterness crept into the young man's voice. He was gazing again at the rails.

In a moment he got to his feet with some unintelligible remark and walked toward the door of the club car.

Rennert gazed for an instant thoughtfully at his back, then idly picked up the magazine which Riddle had left beside his chair. It was a recent number of a popular and sophisticated New York weekly. Rennert's eyes fell on the page which rested uppermost. Probably it was the artist's distorted conception of a Mexican cathedral which prompted him to glance down the lines underneath. They were by a well known columnist, Donald Shaul.

## HARLEQUINADE

TAXCO, June 2. The sun is warm these days in this little mountain-girt Mexican town, and one is satisfied to spend the lazy hours seated upon an iron bench in the plaza gazing alternately at the rose-brown spires of the cathedral and at the groups of fellow expatriates who move about with purposeful step to hide their purposelessness.

For Taxco is this summer the haven of as queer an assortment of expatriate bohemians as ever lent color to a Rive Gauche. They potter aimlessly about the steep cobblestone streets looking, one supposes, for an escape.

Cobblestones are hard walking for feet accustomed to city pavements, however, and the more advanced spirits soon find that one can discuss art and life and one's soul just as well while seated comfortably in a *cantina*. *Tequila*, too, is a great loosener of tongues and inhibitions. When the cantinas became too crowded somebody discovered *marihuana*. For a time everyone smoked the weed and grew lachrymose on visions. But even this has palled now —and what? . . .

Even among such a soul-searching group gossip occasionally crops up, even as in Three Forks, Kansas, or Moscow, Idaho.

Much interest lately has been centered around the still-blonde Gwendolyn Noon, whose spectacular desertion of the footlights of Broadway you may remember (if you remember as far back as the end of last season). Gwendolyn's unexpected action was accounted for at the time by the increasing frequency of unfavorable press notices and by the advent of a young Lochinvar upon the scene.

Lochinvar was handsome and young, still believed in Santa Claus, and his father owned several acres of oil wells out West in Oklahoma. Just what prevented the young knight from carrying off his bride is not known, but for some reason Gwendolyn bought a Spanish dictionary and quietly fared southward to Taxco—unaccompanied. She has spent the time since her arrival here reading good books and dabbling in crystal-gazing.

What's the answer to the riddle, Gwendolyn? Did young Lochinvar's horse shy? Did father have something to say about how sonny boy spent his money? Or is there something to the story that Lochinvar *père* has lost most of his fortune in unwise speculation? Better think it over, Gwen. Half a million in the hand, you know . . .

The magazine was jerked violently from Rennert's hands. He looked up into Riddle's face. The young man stood swaying in front of the doorway and stared at Rennert with narrowed eyes.

"You've been reading that stuff of Shaul's?" he demanded in a hoarse strained voice. "About Gwendolyn Noon, I mean?"

Rennert nodded and said: "Sorry."

Riddle tore the magazine into bits and tossed them far out over the rails. There was a twitching of the muscles of his blood-suffused face as he steadied himself against the railing and watched the pieces of paper flutter and settle slowly to earth.

"It's all a lie!" he spoke through unsteady lips. "He deserves to be killed, the damned——"

He wheeled about and lurched toward the club car.


# CHAPTER TWO

### THE SIAMESE CAT

THE HOUSE WHICH still is known in Taxco as that of Madame Fournier stands upon a steep hillside above and beyond the Little Street of the Hidden Waters. Its roof is of time-dulled red tiles, and its whitewashed adobe walls take on pastel shadings when the sunlight falls upon them. Two wings extend like short, protective arms about a paved terrace, where one may sit and watch the people under the laurel trees in the plaza far below.

The house, in reality, is built in a *barranca* that splits the hill, so that it boasts, as do few houses in Taxco, of two stories. From the terrace one enters a *sala* and finds facing him wide glass doors with the dining room visible beyond. At each end of the long dim sala, are nail-studded doors leading into the apartments on the wings. Between these doors and the dining room tiled stairs ascend to the second floor. Here there are, over the main part of the house, four rooms, and in each of the wings, two.

The house squats, then, in the barranca, like a body, with only the upper part of the torso and the top of the extended arms projecting above the stony sides of the ravine. In any other surroundings it would have a grotesque appearance, like a misshapen cactus in a vase upon a drawing-room table. But in Taxco, where all the houses seem exotic flowering excrescences in the rocks, it is picturesque and at the same time appropriate.

Madame Fournier during her occupancy installed modern plumbing and called the house a pension, so that the discriminating tourist might distinguish it from the many native *casas de huéspedes* in the town. Madame was of French descent; her parents had come to Mexico before the Pastry War, and her father had held a minor position at Maximilian's court. On Bastille Day she always hung out the Tricolor and invited her guests to drink champagne with her. The food at her house was excellent, which fact probably first won the establishment its popularity among visiting foreigners.

Rennert had reserved by letter a large upstairs room in the west wing. The springs of the iron bed were fairly new, the odors of the kitchen did not penetrate this far, and a large window opened upon a particularly attractive vista of red roofs and, in the rainy season, vivid green foliage.

He stood now at the window and gazed with a pleasurably lazy feeling into the mountains. Shadows slanted across the hillsides and bathed the pink and white and ocher houses in warmth. He experienced the same feeling of unreality as always, as if he were standing upon the balcony of a theater and looking down at the backdrop for an operetta, painted in impossibly beautiful colors of scarlet and magenta, of ocher and rose and black. A dream of fairyland—the dream of old José de la Borda —made material by the magic touch of silver.

Yet Taxco, too, had know brutal reality. Along the cobbles of the *camino real* that twists through the town had come armies: Porfirio Díaz, who conscripted the young men of the place. Zapata and his huge-sombreroed horsemen, their eyes on loot. And through it all the painted face of Taxco had changed but little; if anything, had grown more beautiful with age. . . .

Rennert tossed his cigarette through the open window and decided to go down to dinner. He walked along the covered balcony which overlooks the terrace and descended the stairs, at the junction of the wing with the main part of the house.

In the sala, which served as parlor, lounge, and office, Madame Fournier sat in an uncomfortable-looking wooden armchair and folded napkins into mathematically exact rectangles.

Céleste Fournier definitely belonged in that long, narrow room, among the crayon portraits; the paintings of the Virgin of Guadalupe and of La Soledad that flanked the huge crucifix carved in black wood: the long mirrors in rococo gilt frames; the tall whatnots of apple and rosewood cluttered with bric-à-brac of glass and silver filigree and ancient majolica.

The first impression which one got of Madame was that of a general sagging. Her large body sagged comfortably in the chair, as if the broad masculine shoulders had grown weary of supporting their burden. Her black silky-looking dress bulged in unexpected places, so that one suspected a great many layers of other clothing underneath. The lines of her long wedge-shaped face sagged. Her thick, startlingly black eyebrows gave a cavernous effect to her eyes. These were small and black— like two polished buttons—and shrewd and piercing. Only her hair, streaked with gray where it showed beneath a black lace handkerchief, resisted the general settling tendency. It towered above her head like a large unwieldy bun.

As Rennert came down the stairs she looked up and smiled. When she smiled the large mole on the left side of her chin bobbed up and down. To Rennert, there had always been something fascinating about that mole. It did not seem, somehow, to be attached to her skin, but to be capable of animation of its own.

"Good-evening, Mr. Rennert." Her English was a little too liquid. "The room is satisfactory?"

"Yes, madame—as always."

"Few have been here since you were here last spring," she sighed. "Business is not what it used to be. The artists are beginning to go to other places now."

Rennert looked sympathetic.

"You seem to have prospered, though," his clear brown eyes roved over the room. "Some new furniture and, I noticed, a new tub in my bathroom."

"Yes," she nodded, "a few new things."

Rennert stood beside a rosewood cabinet to the right of the doorway and looked through its glass case at the assortment of small stone images and masks which Madame kept for sale to tourists.

"The tourists must have been very *inocentes* and free with their money," he said.

She smiled again.

"As always, señor. But it does not weigh upon my conscience. Back where they come from they say that these things are valuable and ancient, that they themselves have found them in ruined temples. It is money well spent if they can increase their own importance."

Rennert laughed outright. He felt singularly young and carefree, as if he had but needed contact with this plush-darkened room to feel himself in Mexico again. He glanced at the row of fiber masks on the wall above the cabinet and at the ancient musket and bayonet affixed there.

"How many are staying here now?" he asked.

Madame Fournier folded the last napkin and laid it upon the table by her side. The gold Iguala bracelets upon her wrists clinked. (They didn't seem to belong with her, somehow—these bright bracelets. They made her arms look incredibly old and ugly.)

"Seven," she said, "and yourself. There are two ladies—a

Miss Noon and a Mrs. Giddings. You may have heard of Miss
Noon," she glanced up at him. "They say she was once an
actress in New York."

Rennert nodded. His unrenewed acquaintance with the red-
haired young man upon the observation car of the train flashed
into his mind.

Madame Fournier leaned over and gestured toward a thick
ledger that lay upon the table.

"While I think of it, you can register now, if you will be so
kind, Señor Rennert. It is, of course, but a formality."

Rennert picked up an open book that lay face downward
upon the ledger.

"Tennyson's poems." He glanced at her with a quizzical
smile. "Have you gone in for poetry, madame?"

The mole began to bob again.

"No, Señor Rennert, I do not have time for poetry. It is a
book of Mrs. Giddings. She reads much poetry. Here," she
held out her hand, "I will mark her place." She took a sheet
of notepaper from a drawer and inserted it in the book.

Rennert opened the ledger and inscribed his name. He
glanced over the signatures above his.

"The men," Madame Fournier went on, "are more interesting, as always. There is Mr. Shaul, who is writing. He—" she
paused and shrugged—"is not very well liked by the others,
I think. Then there is Dr. Parkyn, who spends his time looking
for jade masks and idols out in the mountains. There is a big
artist named Mandarich, and an American named Crenshaw.
Then there has come this afternoon a young man—another
American. I do not know yet"—her black eyebrows drew together—"why he comes to Taxco. It is not so many, but it fills
the upper floor. And now with Esteban—you remember Esteban, of course?"

Rennert nodded again. Esteban had been the genial black-
eyed youth-of-all-work about the house the spring before.

"He is sick—" Madame Fournier shook her head sadly—
"very sick. I do not know what he has. He suffers from fever
and pains of the stomach. The doctor is with him now." She
sighed again. "It is most inconvenient. I do not know where

to get a new *mozo*. So I must take care of the rooms myself. And this weather! So hot and dry."

"The rains are unusually late in coming, aren't they?"

"Yes, not in all the years that I've lived in Taxco——"

The screaming of a cat cut into her tranquil flow of words. It proceeded from the regions beyond the half-opened door that led into her quarters. It was a screaming shrill yet hoarse and ugly with an undertone of gutturalness.

Rennert looked at her inquiringly.

"What's the matter with Mura?"

Madame had turned in her chair with surprising quickness.

"Ah, you remember Mura, do you? Close the door, will you, so that Esteban will not hear."

Rennert glanced toward the doorway.

The Siamese cat was peering into the sala, her black bat-like ears laid back flat against her head and her large pale-blue eyes, lucent in the dim light, fixed on Rennert's face.

"Mura is not happy these days, *la pobrecita,*" Madame Fournier said as Rennert walked across the room, "she is—how do you say it?—in heat. She wants a husband. But these cats in Taxco, they are not good enough for her, and I do not let her out of the house. I take her to Mexico City soon for a husband who is of royal blood like she is."

As Rennert approached, the cat backed into the dark room beyond, staring at him balefully and growling. Her lithe cinnamon-colored body was trembling. He closed the door upon her savage cries of protest.

"Esteban is asleep?" he asked.

"No." Madame Fournier looked at the scarlet *noche buena* flowers in the bowl by the staircase. "I think that he is awake. But I keep Mura shut up so that he will not hear her again."

"Again?" Something in the woman's tone made Rennert glance at her.

"Yes." She fingered slowly the black wooden beads that hung about her throat. "He is an Indian, you know, and superstitious. Two nights ago he heard her screaming. It frightened him. He has been getting worse ever since."

"You told him what it was?"

She shook her head with slow emphasis.

"Yes, I told him, but he would not believe me. Then I took Mura into his room and showed her to him." She was staring past Rennert's head, and her smile had a queer fixity. "I thought," she said carefully, "that he was dying. I took Mura out of the room."

"The sight of her frightened him?"

"Yes, señor, she frightened him. He did not cry out as a white man would. He just lay and looked at her with those black eyes of his. He said something in a low voice, something that I could not understand. Then he turned his face to the wall. It was then that I thought he was dead. I sent for the doctor. He——" She glanced up at the man who was descending the stairs. "Ah, Mr. Shaul," her manner became suddenly sprightly, "this is Mr. Rennert, who will be with us for a month."

Shaul flicked ashes from the tip of his cigarette into the scarlet flowers and turned sharp dark-brown eyes upon Rennert.

He was a lean, handsome man, probably in his late thirties, with a sallow aquiline face. His shoulders were broad, yet his body, in a loose gray suit of English tweed, looked flabby. He paused, one hand fingering his close-cropped mustache.

"How're you?" He spoke in a quick, inflectionless voice. He made no gesture of extending a hand.

"Glad to know you," Rennert said.

Shaul had turned to Madame Fournier.

"How about a dry Martini?" he said sharply—"out on the terrace. And make it snappy!"

"But yes—" Madame Fournier was getting heavily to her feet—"I will tell María."

"And tell her," Shaul said, "that I need a new candle in my room." He turned toward the door.

"María," Madame explained to Rennert as she gathered up the napkins, "is the daughter of a friend of Micaela, the cook. She is helping me while Esteban is sick."

Shaul had stepped onto the terrace. Rennert, from the doorway, saw him sauntering toward one of the rush-bottomed chairs which stood before the low tile balustrade.

A young man was coming up the steps from the street. It was Riddle, whom Rennert had met on the train two days before.

He paused upon the terrace, then walked up to Shaul and said in a low strained voice: "You're Donald Shaul, I believe?"

The other nodded as he balanced himself gracefully upon the balls of his feet with a slow rhythmical motion. "Well?" he drawled.

Riddle's face was flushed. "My name is Riddle," he said. "I wanted to tell you that you're a damn coward and about the lowest kind of creature that crawls on the earth."

Shaul continued to balance himself, while a faint smile twitched the corners of his thin lips. "So what?" he said in the same tone.

Rennert, standing in the doorway, could see Riddle's face working.

"I'm engaged to Miss Noon," he said. "You're the one who is responsible for her actions since she came down here. You've frightened her—influenced her against me, then double-crossed her by writing about her in that damn lousy column of yours. It's good business for you, I suppose, but——"

Shaul drew the cigarette from his lips and regarded it thoughtfully for an instant. He very carefully flicked it across the balustrade so that it just missed Riddle's face. He turned toward the chair.

As he did so Riddle lunged forward and struck him upon the side of the chin. It was a quick, well-delivered blow and had the force of youthful bone and muscle behind it. Shaul fell. The side of his head struck the balustrade. He crumpled upon the tile floor and lay still.

Rennert walked quickly across the tiles and knelt beside him. He looked up at Riddle, who was standing motionless, his fists still clenched.

"You shouldn't have done that," he said quietly.

Riddle looked dazed.

"No," he said, "I suppose I shouldn't."

# CHAPTER THREE

### THE CAT SCREAMS

"WHAT ABOUT HIM, doctor?" Rennert asked in Spanish. "Is he seriously injured?"

Dr. Otero was very young (his age must not have exceeded twenty-five) and very nervous. His delicate-looking fingers pulled at the cuff of his worn black coat, and he shifted his frail body uneasily from one foot to the other.

"No," he looked at Rennert with close-set obsidian-black eyes and quickly looked away again, "I do not think so, señor. He is unconscious, yes. The blow upon his head—it stunned him. But I think that he will be well very soon."

The sun had sunk behind the mountains, and in the twilight the young man's thin ascetic face looked gray and bloodless.

"Is there anything I can do?" Rennert asked.

"No, I do not think so, señor. There is a young *americana* here in the house who has been helping me with the sick boy downstairs. She will watch this man and see that he is given care when he recovers consciousness. Now," his eyes rested again on Rennert's face, "I must go downstairs again, señor, if you will pardon me."

"What sickness has Esteban?" Rennert asked.

The question seemed to disturb the young Mexican. He fixed his eyes on the wall behind Rennert, and a slight frown crossed his smooth forehead.

"His sickness worries me." He spoke in low, hurried tones, as if to himself. "He has pains in the stomach, señor, and fever. But there is something else that worries me. It is the rash."

"The rash?"

"Yes, on his abdomen and on his chest. It looks——" He checked himself suddenly and inclined his head toward Rennert. "*Con permiso, señor,*" he murmured.

Rennert stood upon the balcony outside Shaul's door and watched the young man's sleek black head and narrow shoulders disappear down the stairs, then followed more slowly.

Above the landing at the top of the stairs hung an antiquated lamp of beaten bronze in which a tiny electric bulb burned feebly.

As he turned to descend the stairs the door upon his left was opened, and a woman stepped upon the balcony. She advanced to the railing and laid a hand upon it as she fixed her eyes appraisingly upon him. Her face was pale against thick ash-blonde hair drawn back from a wide, perfectly contoured forehead. With her left hand she clasped a long cloak of black silk about her lithe svelte body, and Rennert thought that she shivered.

"Tell me," she said, "about Mr. Shaul. Is he seriously injured?" Her voice was low-pitched and had a slight husky quality.

"Not seriously," Rennert answered. "The doctor says that he will probably regain consciousness soon. The blow merely stunned him."

She stood like a black-and-white bas-relief and lifted her chin a bit so that the light fell full upon her face. Her long fingers buried deep-red nails in the silk of the cloak.

"They say that you saw the—the trouble down on the terrace. What happened?"

Rennert was studying her face. It was slightly oval and, except for a very slight prominence of the cheek bones (accentuated now by the drawn look of her skin), of a chiseled perfection of features. Her light hazel eyes were ringed with shadows and had a queer lucent quality about them, as if the pupils were slightly dilated. There was a sallowness underlying her complexion, he saw now, and an air of repressed nervousness about her whole body.

"Riddle came up and expressed his opinion of Shaul, then hit him. As Shaul fell he struck the side of his head against the balustrade. I carried him up to his bedroom. Fortunately, the doctor who is caring for Esteban was in the house at the time."

She leaned forward quickly.

"Did Stephen—Mr. Riddle—mention my name?"

"You are Gwendolyn Noon?"

She nodded, her eyes still fixed on his face.

"Yes," Rennert said, "Riddle accused Shaul of having influenced you against him. He also objected to references to you in Shaul's column."

A look of vexation crossed her face, subtly altering its beauty, and she caught her lower lip between her teeth.

"Oh, the young fool!" she spoke as if to herself. "What did he have to come down here for?"

She stood for a moment, staring fixedly past Rennert's head, then turned and walked to the door of her room. With her hand on the knob, she turned and looked at him again. "Thanks," was all she said as she passed inside.

Rennert walked thoughtfully down the short flight of stairs to the sala and up two steps again into the dining room.

Unshaded ceiling lights cast a stark white glare over the cloths on the small tables and on the whitewashed walls. The floor was of red unglazed tiles and looked damp, as if had been newly washed. The small windows high in the south wall stood open upon the warm Mexican night. Only two of the tables were occupied.

In a corner, watching the little Indian waitress ladle steaming soup from a white tureen, sat a big man in a brown velvet jacket that looked too small for him. His face was large and round, and tortoise-shell glasses lent it a curiously innocent expression. His hair was gray (prematurely gray, it looked) and was cut *en brosse*. He looked up as Rennert entered, then resumed his contemplation of the soup. Rennert glanced at the velvet jacket and the black windsor tie. That, he said to himself, will be the artist whom Madame Fournier mentioned.

Facing the doorway sat Riddle, crumbling a French roll between his fingers and staring at the clay water bottle in the center of the table. His eyes rose as Rennert came in, and he gestured in a vague sort of way. Rennert sat down across from him.

"How's Shaul?" the young man asked without much interest.

Rennert told him of the doctor's words. There was a moment or two of silence when he had concluded.

"I suppose," Riddle laughed grimly, "that I ought to be thankful I didn't kill him." The elaborate care with which his tongue formed the words told the same tales as the empty whisky glass before him.

"In your place, I should be," Rennert said.

"You think that I'm rather an ass for acting the way I did, don't you?" Riddle stared him straight in the face.

Rennert shrugged and said pleasantly: "Not at all. I didn't give a thought to passing judgment on your action. I was merely thinking of the consequences."

"The consequences?"

"You are in Mexico, now, not in the United States."

"You mean about the law?"

"Yes, for one thing."

Riddle's fingers, which had been still, began to crumble bread again.

"I suppose," he said, "that I really ought to tell you all about it, since you seem to have gotten mixed up in it."

"As you wish." Rennert surveyed the menu, on which the dishes that comprised the *cena* had been transcribed painstakingly in green ink.

Riddle rested an elbow on the table and began to move crumbs about with the end of a spoon.

"I met Gwen—Miss Noon—in New York last winter. I took her places and asked her to marry me. She seemed to like me and to be willing to marry me but kept putting it off." He was talking more rapidly now, with no effort to conceal his thickness of tongue. "Finally she said that she was coming down here to Mexico for a time and that as soon as she came back to the United States we would be married."

He paused as the waitress appeared at Rennert's elbow.

"Soon after she came down here to Taxco," he went on when Rennert had given his order, "her letters began to change. She began to write strange things—about the uncertainness of life and all that. It's hard to describe just what I felt in them—a sort of growing coldness. Finally she wrote and hinted that it might be necessary for us to break off our engagement. I had wanted to come down here with her, but"—he fumbled in his pocket for a cigarette—"that was the queerest part of it. She wouldn't let me. Said she wanted to be by herself but that she

would come back as soon as she could. But when I got that last
letter of hers I took the next train to Mexico. I knew that something was wrong." He gestured vaguely with the cigarette.
"You know the rest."

"But I'm afraid," Rennert said over his soup, "that I don't."

"Oh," Riddle seemed confused, "about Shaul, you mean?"

"Yes."

"Well, it's pretty clear, isn't it, that he has been responsible
for the way she has changed her mind? He has influenced her
somehow, maybe got her to break the engagement in order to
make a good bit of gossip for his damn column."

"She *has* broken the engagement, then?" Rennert glanced
at him.

Riddle's lips twitched.

"Yes," he said in a low voice, "definitely. I talked to her this
afternoon. She said that everything was over between us. I
asked her for an explanation, and she said that she had thought
it over and decided that we weren't suited to each other. I'm
sure that damned Shaul is responsible."

"She knew Shaul before she came down here?"

"I don't know, I don't think so."

Rennert considered a moment.

"Of course, it's none of my business," he smiled pleasantly
at Riddle, "but is it true that your father has lost a great deal
of money, as Shaul suggested in his column?"

Riddle flushed angrily.

"Hell, no! It's a damned lie. Dad lost some money in the
stock market, yes. But he still has plenty, more than Shaul will
ever see in *his* life."

He got to his feet abruptly and jammed his hands into his
pockets.

"I think I'll go walk around a while," he said. He paused
awkwardly. "Sorry to have bored you with all this, but I wanted
somebody to talk to." He turned and walked quickly from the
room.


Rennert sat in the little garden at the side of the house and
smoked and listened to Dr. Parkyn talk about jade.

Dr. Parkyn had been sitting beneath the banana palm by the steps leading down to the street when Rennert had come out after dinner. Rennert had been about to retire when the man introduced himself and asked him to sit down in the other chair. He had, Rennert imagined, been sitting there thinking about jade, judging from the way he plunged into the subject.

"One of the many mysteries of Mexico," he was saying in an even, guttural voice whose lack of intonation made it difficult to follow, "is jade. It was very common before the Spanish Conquest, yet no authenticated deposits have been found in modern Mexico. The Aztec tribute books show that it came to Mexico City from the conquered provinces of southwest Mexico, particularly this state of Guerrero in which we now are. Somewhere in these mountains"—he jerked a curved black pipe from the side of his mouth and gestured with it in a semi-circle—"are deposits of jade. I have a theory——"

His theory involved hieroglyphics of place names on Aztec manuscripts, and Rennert did not follow it very closely.

Parkyn's pipe kept going out, and only by means of the continuous lighting of his matches was Rennert able to gain an idea of his features. The sudden glare of the match, emphasizing the stare of his thick-lensed glasses, his angular nose, and his short, bristling mustache, gave his face an aspect of fierce, hawklike immobility. Like, Rennert thought idly, the features of an Assyrian monarch cut in bas-relief upon a temple wall and lit by altar fires. . . .

The sky was overcast, and black clouds banked the horizon, like gigantic projections of the mountain peaks. The night was warm with an electric breathlessness in the atmosphere. Some flower growing by the side of the house gave forth a sweet, intoxicating odor that hung heavy in the air.

The sudden screaming of the Siamese cat cut sharply into Dr. Parkyn's flow of words. It echoed for an instant about the terrace and garden, then died away as suddenly as it had begun.

Dr. Parkyn cleared his throat and said: "Damn that cat!" He bent forward and knocked out his pipe upon the heel of his shoe, then proceeded to refill it.

Rennert looked into the darkness of the mountains that

crouched like dormant beasts about the little town.

"Small wonder," he remarked, "that she frightens Esteban."

"Huh?" Parkyn's eyes were fixed on Rennert's face over the tiny flame of the match which he held above the bowl of his pipe.

"Esteban," Rennert said, "is the boy who works for Madame Fournier——"

"Yes, yes, I know," Parkyn interrupted, "but what was that about the cat frightening him?"

"Just that—the screaming of the cat frightens him."

Parkyn stared now into the flame and drew noisily upon his pipe. He flicked the match to the ground and smoked for a few moments in silence.

"That's one of the most persistent of man's superstitions," he said at last, "the idea that animals are able to sense approaching death. Particularly dogs and cats: doubtless because of their intimate association with man."

"You think that's what is in Esteban's mind?"

"Without a doubt. Esteban is a typical Mexican Indian," Parkyn said in a slow impersonal voice. "He has pigeonholed in his head all the superstitions which his ancestors for centuries back have bequeathed to him. For instance, he wears about his neck a little round stone which he got from a curandera—a witch doctor—to prevent his being hit by *los aires*—the airs. Stones exactly like these have been found in the oldest archæological ruins of Mexico. He went on a trip with me down into the mountains south of here once, down along the Balsas. I had heard that the people of a little village down there kept pre-Conquest idols in their corn cribs, to insure rain and abundant harvests. Before we started, the donkey which we had planned to take with us fell sick. Esteban wouldn't budge a foot until he had looked up a curandera somewhere here in town and got her to burn some copal incense, to ward off further bad luck." He made a noise in his throat that might have been a laugh. "Sure enough, we had a very successful trip. Most of these Mexicans around here have the same beliefs. If old lady Fournier doesn't hurry up and find that cat a mate she will have the whole population of Taxco thinking themselves at the point of death."

"Poor Esteban, I'm afraid he doesn't stand much chance, with the cat foretelling his death and with the administrations of the young fellow who is attending him." Rennert's smile lacked mirth.

"What's the matter with Esteban, anyway?" Parkyn demanded suddenly.

"I asked the doctor this evening," Rennert replied. "To summarize his words—he doesn't know. The boy has pains in the stomach, fever, and a rash on the chest and abdomen."

"A rash?" Parkyn asked quickly.

"Yes. Unfortunately, the regular doctor is away, and his assistant is taking care of Esteban. I doubt whether he knows much more about medicine than do you or I."

Two men were approaching the stone steps that led up to the terrace from the side of the house. As they came into the circle of light from the terrace Rennert recognized Riddle. The young man was walking unsteadily, and his companion was holding to one of his arms.

Riddle paused upon catching sight of Rennert and seemed to be making an effort to regain his poise.

"This," he said with a nod of the head toward the man by his side, "is Mr. Crenshaw, Mr. Rennert."

Crenshaw was a tall, broad-shouldered man wearing a dark suit and a soft hat, the brim of which hid the upper part of his face. Of his features Rennert could distinguish only a square, prognathous chin and a firm, steady mouth.

"Glad to know you," he said. His voice was colorless, and he clipped his words off sharply.

"Mr. Rennert," Riddle explained thickly, "is one of the guests here. I met him on the train coming down."

Crenshaw made no comment. Rennert had the feeling that he was being studied rather closely.

"How are you, Crenshaw?" Parkyn spoke from the chair.

"All right," Crenshaw answered briefly, with a glance into the shadows beneath the banana palm.

Rennert felt that introductions were getting rather tangled. He said: "This is Mr. Riddle, Dr. Parkyn."

They nodded. Parkyn made no motion to rise.

"Do you know," Crenshaw addressed Parkyn, "why there's a soldier stationed in the street below here?"

"A soldier? No, I don't."

Riddle laughed too loudly.

"He watched us as if we were suspicious characters, asked us if we were staying in this house."

They stood for a moment in awkward silence. Riddle laughed again.

"Let's put it to bed, Riddle," Crenshaw said, in a voice that just missed being peremptory.

"All right," Riddle lurched forward, "might as well, I guess."

Rennert sat down and listened to the murmur of their voices upon the terrace. Riddle was talking volubly.

"What did you say that young fellow's name was?" Parkyn asked.

"Riddle, he's from somewhere in Oklahoma—Tulsa, I believe."

He heard Parkyn's teeth click very distinctly against the stem of his pipe.

"Riddle? The son of Owen Riddle, the oil man?"

"I believe," Rennert said, "that his father is interested in oil. I only met this young fellow on the train the other day."

"What's he doing down here?" Parkyn asked after a moment.

"I don't know," Rennert said.

Parkyn tapped his pipe upon the heel of his shoe again.

"I have some letters to write before the lights are turned out," he said, rising. "This business of turning off the electricity at eleven o'clock may be conducive to peace and quiet but not to industry."

"In a few more years," Rennert laughed, "the night clubs will be here. Better enjoy Taxco's unmarred quiet while we may."

"Yes, yes." Parkyn seemed preoccupied. "Well, see you in the morning."

Rennert bid him good-night and sat for a while, savoring the last of his cigar and staring at the scattered lights upon the hills.

His thoughts, somehow, kept returning to young Riddle. And to the blonde Gwendolyn Noon. She was rather baffling. Why had she broken the engagement with the youngster? Because she believed the rumor that his father had suffered financial reverses? Or was there, as Riddle insisted, some other influence at work? She had certainly insisted on postponing the marriage with him until the return from Taxco before the rumor about the money losses started. Or had she? There was, the thought came to Rennert suddenly, one explanation for her visit to Mexico which might account for a great deal. . . .

He yawned (*Five hours in Taxco,* he told himself happily, *and I'm all ready for bed at nine-thirty*), tossed away the stub of his cigar, and decided to turn in.

The bronze lamp over the stairs cast a pool of light upon the landing but left the balcony a place of gently moving shadows that deepened into darkness beyond the door of Rennert's room.

He stood with his hand on the knob and looked at the thin pencil of light that slanted across the tiles a few feet beyond him. Shaul's door stood slightly ajar. Thinking that the columnist had recovered consciousness, he walked along the balcony and tapped gently upon the panel.

There was no response from within. After a momentary hesitation he pushed the door open and looked inside.

The unshaded electric bulb illuminated the sheets and the upturned face of the man who lay upon the bed against the opposite wall. Halfway between the head of the bed and the door a woman was standing still and staring at him. A black dress sheathed her tall angular body. Her dark brown hair was cut in a severely mannish bob, and her features were thin and rather pinched-looking. Her lips were thin, and she held them pressed very firmly together. Her hands (their delicate fragility contrasted startlingly with the severity of her appearance) were laid flat against the white apron she wore.

For some reason her first words surprised Rennert. Perhaps it was because of her voice. She said, "Who are you?" in a quiet matter-of-fact tone.

"I have the room next to this," Rennert explained. "I saw a light in here and thought that perhaps Shaul had regained consciousness. I came in to see if I might be of some assistance."

There was a momentary pause; then her eyes left his and sought the bed.

"You are too late," she said dispassionately. "He is dead."

# CHAPTER FOUR

## QUARANTINE

R ENNERT STEPPED forward and leaned over the bed.

Shaul's face. beneath the bandages which covered his forehead, seemed to have lost some of its sharpness. It looked puffy; there was a bluish tinge to his skin, and his lips were swollen. The covers were drawn up to a level with his shoulders. and his hands lay beneath them, one flung over his breast, the other stretched at his side.

Rennert straightened up and faced the woman.

"I am Mrs. Giddings," she said, "one of the guests here. I have been nursing the sick boy downstairs and told the doctor that I would take care of Mr. Shaul. I came in just now to see if he had regained consciousness. I found him like this—dead."

Her eyes (large, dark brown, and of a liquid beauty that one noticed only on second glance) were still fixed upon the bed, and there was a puzzled frown on her face.

"The doctor is downstairs with Esteban," she said hastily. "I'll call him. You will remain here?"

"Yes."

· She moved softly across the floor on her low-heeled shoes and disappeared onto the balcony.

Rennert glanced about the room. It was like the other rooms in Madame Fournier's pension. Whitewashed walls, bare of ornament save for a small crucifix, carved in dark wood, upon the wall over the bed. The floor of large red unglazed tiles. A cheap wooden washstand upon which stood a large new candle in a black Oaxaca urn, and a Puebla jar filled with pink and red carnations. A small desk against the wall which separated this from Rennert's own room. Three rush-bottomed chairs with painted wooden backs. At the window long starched white curtains edged with coarse hand-made lace.

Rennert's gaze came back to the bed. He was experiencing a feeling of regret, not so much for the man who lay there as for young Riddle. There was no telling what attitude the Mexican authorities might take about Shaul's death. They would doubtless make it exceedingly unpleasant for the young man. At least there would be legal machinery which would move slowly and require considerable greasing. . . .

As he thought, he was gazing down at Shaul's face. The weak light from the unshaded electric bulb bathed his features. His eyes stared upward at the ceiling. Their pupils seemed greatly contracted, reduced to mere pinpoints. His lips and throat were discolored by tiny crimson and purple spots. The edge of the bandage upon his forehead was tinged with still damp blood.

Rennert suddenly bent forward, but straightened himself as the door opened.

The young Mexican doctor came hurriedly into the room, nodded perfunctorily to Rennert, and approached the bed.

Rennert, as he watched him, was aware that Mrs. Giddings had followed him in and was standing by the dresser, her eyes intent on his actions.

In a few moments the doctor turned to them and shrugged.

"Yes," he said, "he is dead. I shall notify the authorities at once so that the body may be removed in the morning." He spoke in quick staccato Spanish.

"But, Dr. Otero, it was my understanding that he was not seriously injured," Mrs. Giddings said very quietly in halting Spanish. "He was resting well when I saw him last, and the wound on his head did not appear to be serious." As she spoke her eyes were resting on the bed, and there was in them the same puzzled look.

The doctor frowned and twisted a ring upon one of his fingers. The large opal in it flashed in the light.

"These wounds of the head," he said nervously, "it is difficult to tell about them, señora. This one will have been more serious than we thought." He stood for a moment in agitated silence. "I must go now," he said, with a quick bow in her direction.

He walked quickly to the door and went out.

Mrs. Giddings made a motion as if to follow him but paused, her eyes on Rennert's face.

The room was very still and through the open window came the sound of singing down by the plaza. It was a serenade, and of the words *"tus ojos"* alone were distinguishable. They came in melancholic repetition, their insistence emphasized by the faint tinkle of a guitar.

For a long moment they gazed at each other, her eyes clear and bright, with a queer look of uncertainty, his sharply speculative.

"Is there something wrong?" he asked.

She drew a long breath and parted her lips, though for a moment she did not speak.

"I don't know," she said at length, "whether there is or not. It probably isn't important."

"What is it?"

A trace of animation crept into her voice. "There is something about this bed," she moved closer to it. "It's this pillow."

There were two small pillows upon the bed. Upon one, at the opposite side, lay Shaul's head. The nearer was smooth and unruffled. It was to this pillow that she pointed.

"When I was in his room last, that pillow was under his head—but it was turned the other way."

"The other way?"

"Yes, the other side on top."

Rennert bent over the bed. "You are sure?"

"Yes, I know, because I arranged them for the night." She stood beside him and lifted the end of the pillowcase between thumb and forefinger. "You see, these are monogrammed on one side only. When I left this room the monogrammed side lay upwards. Now it is turned down."

Rennert picked up the pillow carefully and held it to the light. The monogram was a small ornate "F," worked in blue thread. Near the other end of the case was a faint streak of red.

His face was grave as his eyes went from the pillow to the still face upon the bed and to the fringe of blood upon the bandage. He laid the pillow upon the bed in its former position and was straightening up when a sound upon the balcony outside the door made him glance in that direction. He stepped quickly past Mrs. Giddings and looked up and down the narrow expanse of tiles. There was no one in sight. Somewhere below two men were talking in low, excited tones.

"What is it?" The woman was staring at him.

"I thought that I heard someone upon the balcony. You heard nothing?"

She shook her head.

"It must have been down on the terrace. I heard nothing."

Rennert stood for a moment upon the threshold, thoughtfully.

"What rooms," he asked, "open upon this balcony?"

"The next one is yours, of course. Then comes mine, and then Miss Noon's. Those are all."

Rennert came into the room and closed the door carefully behind him.

"When did you leave this room the last time?" he asked in a low voice.

Mrs. Giddings stood with her hands thrust into the pockets of her white apron. The attitude gave her a curiously masculine appearance.

"At about eight-thirty," she stated, the animation gone from her voice. "I came up here to look at Mr. Shaul, I stayed not more than three or four minutes, just long enough to see that he was resting easily."

"He was alive then?"

"Oh, yes, unconscious but alive. His pulse was becoming normal again, his breathing was regular, and I expected him to regain consciousness at any moment. I returned just now—and found him dead."

Their eyes met.

"Do you know of anyone who came here after your visit?" Rennert asked.

"No, I was in my room, resting. I may have dropped off to sleep."

"Do you notice anything else about this room that has changed? Anything at all, however insignificant?"

Her eyes traveled slowly about her, then she shook her head.

"No, nothing except that pillow, but I probably wouldn't notice it if there were anything else, since I was only in here once before and then only for a few moments." She stared down at the bed. "Of course, it's all very simple about that pillow. Mr. Shaul must have regained consciousness after I left and moved it. But still," she paused, "it struck me as strange."

"But if he had regained consciousness would you have expected him to die so soon?"

"No," she said slowly, "not—not naturally." He had the feeling that the calmness of her voice was due to control.

"And," Rennert kept his eyes fixed on her face, "the pillow has been smoothed out. A man in the throes of death wouldn't do that."

"No," she said, "he wouldn't."

Down by the plaza the serenade had stopped, and the night was very still outside the open window.

"There is only one explanation for that pillow, then?" In the pulsing stillness that seemed to have settled upon the room her voice sounded strangely far away.

"I am afraid," Rennert said, "that there is only one. I wondered when I saw his face closely. The contraction of the pupils of his eyes and the spots on the skin due to extravasation about the pillow seems to leave no doubt."

A slight tremor passed over her body, and Rennert observed that she thrust her hands deeper into the pockets of the apron.

"What shall we do?" she asked through tight lips.

Down by the plaza the serenader had begun again, this time farther away, so that the sounds of his voice and guitar mingled almost imperceptibly with the countless tiny noises of the night.

For a long time Rennert did not reply. The bluish tinge of Shaul's skin combined with the distortion of his swollen lips to lend an unpleasantly feral look to his face. The sneering half-smile which Rennert had seen down upon the terrace seemed still to linger about those lips. In contrast, Taxco's quiet flow of existence seemed more inviting than ever. And Rennert felt tired in body and spirit.

"I am tempted," he said slowly, "to do nothing."

He felt the woman's eyes fixed on his face.

"But," he looked up at her and laughed grimly, "I shall, of course. After all, if we are right, it is murder."

She nodded, and her face looked haggard, older in the weak light.

"Yes," she said, "it is only people who do not have consciences who can take life easily."

Rennert looked once more at the face upon the bed, then turned away.

"And unless I am mistaken," he said, "Donald Shaul was such a person."

As if by common agreement they made their way to the door. Rennert stopped to turn off the light and closed the door behind them.

Upon the balcony the night air seemed to have grown cooler. They walked in silence to the stairs. Halfway down the flight Mrs. Giddings, who was still slightly in advance, stopped abruptly and stared down into the sala.

"Who is that standing with Dr. Otero?" Her voice was low and tense, as if surprise had momentarily loosened her control.

Rennert descended another step and stood by her side.

Standing between the dining-room door and the foot of the stairs was a small man who wore, unmistakably, the faded uniform of the Mexican army. A revolver was strapped at his side. He looked up and, with a word to the young doctor who stood beyond him, advanced to the foot of the stairs. He halted stiffly, and his quick black eyes met Rennert's.

"The Señor does not intend to leave the house?" he said in Spanish.

"No," Rennert answered, "not since you are here. I should like to speak to you in private for a few moments."

"But no, it is impossible now," the man seemed excited. "There is much to be done. I have not time to talk with you now."

"It is a case of death," Rennert said.

"Of death, of course, señor. You mean the man who has died upstairs. The doctor has told of him. That is unfortunate, yes, but it must wait. This other affair is more important now."

Rennert's eyes narrowed. *"Qué pasa?"* he asked quickly.

"It is the quarantine, señor."

"The quarantine?"

"But yes," the soldier's voice took on a ring of authority, "this house is under the quarantine. No one is allowed to leave for the present."

"It is Esteban, the mozo?"

"Yes, señor, the doctor says that he has the measles or perhaps—" he hesitated—"the smallpox."

Behind him Rennert heard Mrs. Giddings' sharp intake of breath. He was thinking rapidly and feeling, despite himself, a quickening of the pulse.

"And when," he asked, "was this quarantine declared?"

The soldier hesitated.

"An hour ago, señor, but we did not announce it until all the guests were within the house for the night. We wished," he shrugged, "to avoid any unpleasantness."

"And no one has been allowed to leave this house during that time?"

"No one, señor. Soldiers have been on guard upon the street."

"You have been in the house during the past hour?"

"Yes, señor." The man's eyes were fixed sharply on Rennert's face.

"Did you see anyone go up or come down this staircase?"

Thinly veiled hostility was in the Mexican's voice as he replied stiffly: "It was not my duty to watch the staircase, señor." He glanced toward the doorway as another uniformed figure appeared upon the terrace, inclined his head toward Mrs. Giddings, and left them.

Dr. Otero stood upon the steps that led up to the dining room and watched Rennert. His face looked ashen. He approached diffidently.

"You asked," he said in a low voice, "if he had seen anyone upon that staircase. I saw a man go up those stairs, señor."

"You did?" Rennert studied him. "Did you know him?"

"No, señor, I am not acquainted with the guests in this house. I was but passing through the sala and saw him. He was a young man with red hair. He came down the other staircase, crossed the sala, and went up the stairs where the señora is standing now."

"When did he come down?"

The man shrugged his thin shoulders.

"I cannot say, señor, I was but passing through the room."

"And what time was this?"

"After the nines, señor, perhaps fifteen minutes, I am not sure." He stood for a moment, watching Rennert's face, then inclined his head. "The señor knows the young man?" he asked.

Rennert nodded.

"With your permission, then, I shall leave you." Dr. Otero walked past them and opened softly the door that led into the room beyond the stairs, the room where, Rennert surmised, Esteban lay.

He and Mrs. Giddings stood in silence upon the lower treads of the stairs. The woman's eyes were fixed upon the shadows by a tall whatnot in the corner. The little remaining color seemed to have drained from her face, leaving it more pinched-looking than ever.

"You left Shaul's room at approximately eight-thirty?" Rennert asked.

"Yes," she raised her eyes very slowly to his face. In their steady unblinking stare Rennert saw a slow look of horror appear.

"And you are positive that he was alive then?"

"Yes, positive." Again the tremor passed over her body, and with one hand she reached for the railing.

Rennert stepped toward her.

She laughed with forced lightness. "Don't worry, Mr. Rennert, I'm not the kind of woman who faints. It was just that the conclusion struck me rather—forcibly."

"I think, Mrs. Giddings, that for tonight at least you had best keep your suspicions to yourself." Rennert's voice was urgent. "In the morning we shall see what can be done."

"Then," she said with rigid calmness, "I am right?"

"Yes," Rennert said, "you are doubtless right. This unexpected clamping down of the quarantine makes it rather certain that the murderer of Shaul is still in this house."

She turned back up the stairs.

"At least," she laughed grimly, "one feels safer with soldiers about."

Rennert ascended the stairs after her and walked thoughtfully along the balcony to his room. He opened the door and pressed a finger against the light-button beside it.

There came no answering illumination.

He stood for a moment staring into the darkness, then struck a match and walked to the dresser where stood one of Madame Fournier's massive yellow candles in a black Oaxaca urn. He lit the candle and carried it to the center of the room. He held it up to the pendant light bulb. He placed his fingers carefully about the top of the bulb and turned it.

Weak yellow light flooded the room.

Rennert blew out the candle and replaced it upon the dresser.

He remembered the noise upon the balcony as he and Mrs. Giddings had stood beside Shaul's bed. He pictured the person who had stood there hastily taking refuge in this, the next room, and, in case he should enter it in his search, unscrewing the light bulb. The idea had probably been to escape onto the balcony as he walked to the dresser for the candle. He thought, glancing at the light bulb: *"I wonder just how cool-headed this person was?"*

He stood for a moment, analyzing the insistent feeling of uneasiness that nagged at him. His face was grave as he left the room and walked down the balcony. He knocked very softly at Mrs. Giddings' door, and when she opened it he said: "Pardon the melodrama, but I thought that I ought to warn you to be careful tonight."

"Careful?" she stared at him.

"Yes. I am afraid that someone overheard our conversation about the pillowcase." He told of the unscrewed light-bulb in his room. "At present there is only your testimony to indicate that Shaul did not die as a result of the blow upon his head. You constitute, then, what is called a star witness. Things sometimes happen to star witnesses."

Her laugh was ineffective.

"That key looks as if it had kept malefactors out of women's bedchambers for centuries." She glanced down at the massive lock. "I'll be sure that it is turned when I go to bed."

Rennert's eyes were resting upon the door at the other side of the room.

"Unless I am mistaken," he said, "the rooms in this part of the house are arranged upon the suite plan. There is another room beyond your bath?"

"Yes, Miss Noon's room is beyond."

Rennert's voice was urgent. He said: "Be sure that the door from the bath into your room is locked before you go to bed."


# CHAPTER FIVE

### THE DOOR BETWEEN

M ADAME FOURNIER stood at the door and listened. No sound came from the other side of the thick wooden panel, yet she knew that someone was standing in the dark sala. Standing on the tiles in front of her door and, like herself, listening.

Fear made Madame Fournier sick. For two days she had been able to eat but little, and the consequent faintness made all the worse the panic that was sweeping over her in recurrent waves. It was a feeling which she had never experienced before. Even that day when Zapata and his horsemen dashed into Taxco, she had been concerned not so much with her personal safety as with that of her possessions. This, she imagined, was the way one felt in a severe earthquake, with the ground ready to yawn open at one's feet.

She bent forward suddenly and applied her ear to the wood. She was positive that she had heard low hurried breathing out in the sala. It had stopped now, however, and the silence throughout the house was absolute. There were not even any of those myriad unidentified little noises that old houses make at night.

Madame Fournier wondered if prayer would help, and her fingers stole upward to the tiny gold crucifix which hung at her breast. She had always worn it, this little crucifix, much as she had worn black lace and a *rebozo*. It had constituted one of the countless little grooves in which one's life ran and which one took for granted. Madame attended an occasional mass and, mostly for policy, paid a small yearly contribution to the *parroquia*. Sometimes, when she was tired, she experienced a pleasurable feeling of something approaching awe in the vast candlelit interior of Santa Prisca's church. At heart, though, she had always known these stiff gaudily dressed images of tortured saints for what they were—plaster playthings that justified the contribution box. Now, she wasn't so sure, and at the thought that hell might conceivably be something more than a priestly fiction a queer sensation of coldness went through her body.

As padded feet scurried across the tiles behind her she actually slumped forward on her knees and barely resisted the impulse to scream. She knelt there for a moment, scarcely breathing. When she turned, the eyes of the Siamese cat were staring at her through the darkness with unblinking fixity. Mura was silent, as if from temporary exhaustion, and her eyes seemed two bright objects disembodied.

Madame Fournier got to her feet and picked up the candle from the chair beside the door. She stood there for a long time, holding a match in one hand and the Oaxaca urn in the other. She was undecided. She wanted to light the candle, throw open the door, and face the visitor who, she was sure, stood in the sala. Anything, she thought, to stop this eternal nerve-racking vigilance. There was, on the other hand, the possibility that this person was armed. Madame Fournier considered the matter and decided that in all probability this would be true—this time. She remembered suddenly the old musket and bayonet which hung on the wall of the sala, above the row of Aztec masks. She had used the bayonet once to kill a snake which had lain coiled upon the terrace. Suppose the person who would face her in case she opened the door held this bayonet in those hands whose strength she had already felt. The thought nauseated her, and she wanted to breathe some fresh cool air. (Madame Fournier slept these nights with tightly closed windows. She had even driven nails through the frames, to fix them more securely in place.) The desire for air became all at once uncontrollable, dispelling fear. She struck the match against the door and lit the candle.

Light reassured her, and she swiftly turned the key in the lock. She opened the door and held up the candle. There was no one in sight. Madame Fournier stood for a long time, gulping avidly the night air and staring into the shadows about the stairway on the other side of the room.

## CHAPTER SIX

### BY CANDLELIGHT

THE SCREAMING of the Siamese cat awoke Rennert to abrupt startled consciousness. It seemed for an instant to pervade the house, then ended as suddenly as it had begun, on a high frenetic note. In the utter silence that followed he could hear distinctly the soft dispassionate ticking of his watch upon the table by the bed.

He sat up and groped for his cigarettes. He lit one and lay staring into the darkness of the window that was flanked by long white curtains that dragged the floor.

The room felt close and musty, and he had the strange feeling that the curtains were blocking the entry of air. He had attained that alertness of the senses which comes sometimes after abrupt awakening in the night and which is followed so soon by deeper slumber.

He found that thoughts of that night kept returning with irritating persistence. It was not so much the fact that a man had died in the room next to him (he was rather thick-skinned about matters like that) so much as an interest in the problem presented by the little group of strangely assorted people assembled under Madame Fournier's tiled roof. The evidence of the pillow convinced him that one of them had stolen into Shaul's room and finished the job which young Riddle had begun out on the terrace. Riddle himself? Somehow or other Rennert found himself reluctant to associate the red-haired young fellow with a crime of this sort, despite the evidence of Dr. Otero that he had seen him ascend the stairs to this wing. His temper aroused, Riddle might well be capable of killing a man openly, but to steal upon him while he lay unconscious—that was a different matter. Who, then? To his knowledge—extremely limited knowledge, he admitted—there was only one other person in the house who might have a motive for doing away with the columnist: Gwendolyn Noon . . .

He reached over to crush out his cigarette. Yes, he admitted to himself, Shaul's death might very well have been accomplished by a woman. It would not have required much strength, it might not have been premeditated (his fingers firmly ground the tobacco into the tray). A chance errand to Shaul's room . . .

From the next room came a thud, as of wood against wood.

Rennert threw back the covers, put on a dressing gown and slippers, and walked quickly to the door. He stepped out upon the balcony. The light at the head of the stairs had been extinguished, and the balcony and the terrace lay in silence and darkness. Somewhere, far off in the mountains, a dog was howling lugubriously.

He stepped to the door of Shaul's room and threw it open.

The flame of the candle in the black Oaxaca urn upon the floor trembled in the draft and slowly righted itself.

Beside it stood Gwendolyn Noon.

About her she clasped the same loose cloak which she had worn earlier in the night. Against its blackness the deep-red nails of her left hand were like so many tiny gaping wounds. Her right hand was buried beneath its folds, so that her sleeve fell back, just revealing an angry bruise upon her elbow. She stood very still and stared at him. The candle flame, lighting her face from below, made her eyes look large and clear, and again Rennert had the sensation that they were slightly dilated.

For a moment neither spoke.

Then her lips twitched as with a nervous tic she closed and opened her eyes in a quick automatic movement and laughed forcedly.

"Rather a melodramatic meeting, isn't it, Mr. Rennert?"

Rennert smiled and looked down at the shallow urn in which stood the tall newly lit candle. It could not have been burning, he estimated by the wax running down the sides, more than four or five minutes.

"Yes," he said, "all the required elements of melodrama—the hour of midnight or thereabouts, the woman, and"—his eyes were resting upon the wrinkled black fragments in the bottom of the urn—"the papers—the ubiquitous papers."

She laughed again with the same lack of mirth and stepped backward to lean against the small desk which stood against the wall separating this room from his.

Rennert stooped and picked up the urn. The candle, set loosely upon the bottom of the pottery, swayed. He caught it and let some of the wax drip downward. He pressed the end of the candle into it and set the urn upon the desk beside the woman. As he did so he was observing her closely, noticing the slight twitching of her shoulders, the furtive manner in which her eyes avoided his, the way in which the right hand remained buried in the folds of her cloak. He saw that she kept her eyes averted from the bed, where lay Shaul's sheet-covered figure.

She made no obvious effort to regain control of herself and tossed back her hair from her forehead with a quick imperious gesture.

"I suppose," she said, "that you are curious to know what I am doing in this room in the middle of the night."

"Curious, naturally, Miss Noon, but it is really none of my business."

Her eyes rested on his, and he saw a slowly calculative look come into them. She leaned forward slightly.

"You will not say anything about it, then—to anyone?" Her voice was almost a whisper.

He regarded her steadily for a moment.

"I cannot promise that, Miss Noon, but I shall not do so unless I find it my duty—and I assure you that my sense of duty is not very strong in some cases."

"What do you mean?" Her eyes were wandering about the room again, as if reluctant to rest.

"I was thinking," he said, "about Riddle."

"About Riddle? What about him?"

"I suppose you realize that Shaul's death puts him in a rather difficult position?"

"Yes," she was staring fixedly at the candle flame, "I suppose it does. He will be held responsible, I suppose?"

"Probably. If he is, I think that you should give some explanation for your visit to this room."

Her eyes narrowed slowly so that her face in profile lost some of its chiseled beauty.

"But my coming here tonight has no connection with Shaul's death."

"It may," Rennert said evenly, "have more connection than you think."

She continued to stare with curious concentration at the candle.

"What did Riddle tell you—about us?" she asked suddenly, drawing her cloak more closely about her.

"He has told me of his meeting with you in New York, of his——"

Rennert's hesitation was momentary but she supplied quickly: "Go ahead and say it: infatuation."

"Yes," Rennert said evenly, "I was about to say 'infatuation.' You must remember that my viewpoint is necessarily that of the casual observer."

"It makes no difference," she waved her left hand with a sudden impulsive gesture.

"Riddle is unable to understand why you came to Mexico instead of marrying him at once. He is also unable to account for your breaking off the engagement, and, quite naturally, perhaps, he blames Shaul."

"He's right—" her voice hardened, became edged with bitterness—"Shaul *was* responsible."

"And now?" Rennert suggested quietly.

He thought that her right hand tightened under the folds of her cloak.

"Now," she spoke with slow emphasis, "things are different."

"You have told Riddle so?"

"I have not seen him since—" she glanced furtively at the bed—"since Shaul died. I'm going to tell him tomorrow."

"That you have decided not to break your engagement with him?"

"Yes."

"I should advise you to tell Riddle also the reason for your visit to this room tonight and for your coming to Mexico."

She sank back against the desk and put out a hand to steady herself. It struck the edge of the urn. The candle fell against its side and leaned, guttering, while wax dripped slowly upon the surface of the table. She reached out and righted the candle, her fingers stark white and vivid red against the soft yellow wax.

"Then you know why I came to Taxco?" she asked without looking up.

"I think that I do," Rennert's eyes were on her fingers and on the candle. "Many others have come for the same reason."

She was staring now at her finger tips and gently rubbing them against each other.

"Shaul told you?" she asked.

"No, it is merely a guess."

"Riddle doesn't suspect?"

"I am sure that he does not."

"You think," she asked, "that he might find it out—after we were married?"

"You have been on the stage," Rennert said. "Isn't that a stock situation for plays?"

Her lips parted slightly, and she stood up.

"Maybe you're right." She looked him full in the face. "I'll think it over, anyway. After—" her mouth and throat suddenly twitched as if an electric shock had passed over her face—"after I get some sleep."

Rennert stood aside.

"You finished your errand in this room, Miss Noon?"

She was moving toward the door, her scarlet silk mules brushing softly against the tiles.

"Yes," she said, "I can finish what I have to do in my room."

Rennert stepped to the door and held it open for her. She paused upon the threshold and stared for a moment at the floor. When she looked up her eyes were queer and sharp, as if in alarm at a sudden thought.

"You seem to have an interest in this, some way," she spoke very clearly and evenly. "I hope that you are not going to imitate Shaul."

Rennert watched her disappear into the darkness of the balcony.

As he stood there at the door he glanced across the terrace to the other balcony. Near the railing at the head of the stairs he saw the faint glow of a cigarette. Even as he watched, it was flipped outward to fall in a wide spiral to the terrace floor. Across the stillness there came to his ears the closing of a door.

He stood for a moment, staring thoughtfully into the darkness, then turned back into Shaul's room. He blew out the candle and picked up the Oaxaca urn in which it stood. He thought as he carried it along the balcony to his room: *I think that the fingerprints of Shaul's murderer are upon the wax of this candle.*

# CHAPTER SEVEN

## SUNLIGHT ON THE TILES

THE SOLDIER in the nondescript faded uniform who stood upon the sun-bathed terrace looked very young and not a little ludicrous in his self-conscious wearing of the air of authority; but the revolver strapped at his side looked very serviceable. It injected a note of grim reality against the painted backdrop of Taxco.

The soldier's hand was upon the butt of this revolver now as he faced the large man in leather jacket, riding breeches, and boots. This man grasped under one arm a large portfolio and

was gesticulating and speaking in a painstaking mixture of
Spanish and English which seemed utterly incomprehensible
to his vis-à-vis.

Rennert heard the voices as he descended the stairs to a late
breakfast. He stepped to the front door.

The large man who stood with his back to him was the
owner of the gray hair, the tortoise-shell glasses, and the moon-
like face whom he had seen in the dining room the night before. Upon his head he wore now a wide-brimmed black hat,
pulled sideways at a rakish angle.

He turned as Rennert came to the door, and a childish look
of relief came over his face.

"Do you speak Spanish?" he asked in a deep resonant voice
that fitted poorly with his appearance.

"Yes." Rennert stepped forward.

"Then please come here and find what in the hell this fellow
is saying to me. He doesn't seem to want me to leave the
house."

"I think I can tell you beforehand," Rennert said. He exchanged a few words in Spanish with the soldier and turned
to the man, who was tapping the toe of a boot impatiently
against the tiles.

"You are right," he said, "that he objects to your leaving
the house. It is under quarantine, and none of us are allowed
to leave the premises for the present."

"Quarantine?" the other repeated blankly, his blue eyes
squinting behind the huge glasses. "Nonsense, why should the
house be quarantined?"

"It is Esteban, the Mexican boy who works for Madame
Fournier," Rennert explained. "The doctor decided last night
that he had the measles."

"Measles?" the other laughed. "Why, I had them when I
was a kid."

"Unfortunately, the young man who is attending Esteban is
not certain that it *is* the measles. He says that it may be the
smallpox. Smallpox is a *bête noir* among Mexicans."

"Damn!" The full force of Rennert's words seemed to strike
him all at once, and he stared past the soldier down the hillside.

"I was going down towards Iguala today to paint. This is a nuisance."

"As to that," Rennert smiled, "I think everyone is in agreement."

"How long is this quarantine likely to last?"

Rennert shrugged in the best Mexican manner.

"The regular doctor is expected back tomorrow or the next day. He will be able then to tell what is wrong with the boy. In the meantime there is nothing to do except wait."

The other brought his eyes back to Rennert's face. There was something disconcerting about his steady, unblinking stare. Then he squinted suddenly and said: "Well, I suppose one might as well take it philosophically. This hillside," he waved a pudgy hand out over the terrace, "hasn't been painted more than a dozen times. I might as well do it again." He deposited the portfolio upon a chair and turned back toward the doorway. Just inside it he paused and addressed Rennert.

"You are staying here, I take it?" -

Rennert nodded.

"My name's Mandarich." The other stepped across the threshold and extended a hand.

Rennert introduced himself and shook hands. Mandarich's hand felt soft and unpleasantly moist, although there was in his fingers a surprising strength.

"I'll probably be seeing you often around here, since neither of us can leave," Mandarich said as he turned back into the sala. He crossed it, and Rennert heard his heavy boot-clad feet ascending the right staircase.

Rennert turned to the soldier, who had been regarding them with a stolid face.

"The officer in charge here," he inquired politely, "who is he?"

"El Capitán Pérez, señor." The black eyes stared into his.

"He will come to the house this morning?"

"Yes, señor, I think so."

Rennert tendered a card beneath which a folded five-peso bill was partially concealed.

"Will you have the kindness of giving him this card when

he comes? My room is the middle one on the west wing upstairs."

"*Como no, señor,*" the soldier quickly pocketed the card and the bill.

Rennert walked through the sala into the dining room. It was deserted and had that peculiarly cheerless appearance which Mexican dining rooms invariably possess. The windows were tightly closed and the air felt close and musty, pervaded by the smell of garlic.

He sat down at a table and surveyed idly the menu of the evening before, which had not yet been removed.

It was several minutes before a small and frightened-looking Indian girl peered out of the kitchen and timidly approached his table. She took his order and whisked away.

Loud staccato voices from the kitchen fell upon his ears, and in a moment Madame Fournier appeared.

She was breathing heavily, with a faint asthmatic wheeze, and was clasping a black rebozo about her shoulders. Her hair had lost something of its careful coiffure and straggled from beneath the lace cap, which was set awry upon her head. Powder streaked her face, emphasizing rather than hiding the sagging lines and the dark pouches beneath her eyes. She approached Rennert's chair and laid a heavily ringed hand upon the back of it. She sighed.

"Señor," her tone was motherly—forcedly so, Rennert felt, "a thousand pardons for the delay. But the house—it is turned upside down this morning. You have heard of the quarantine?"

Rennert nodded.

"*Mon Dieu!*" she plucked at the fringe of the rebozo. "It will ruin me! Who will come now to my house? And how to take care of those who are here? The cook is afraid and thinks that she feels the hand of the disease upon her. She is drinking some heathen mixture of herbs. The girl María knows nothing about the work. And there is no way to get other servants. I must do everything myself, even attend to the rooms. I, at my age!" She paused as if for breath.

Rennert extended his sympathy.

"How is Esteban this morning?" he asked.

"Worse, señor, worse." She shook her head slowly and stared through the doorway while the fingers of her left hand busied themselves with her beads. "He will not take the medicine which the doctor gives him. And," her voice dropped to a whisper, "I think that he listens for something all the time."

"Listens?" Rennert glanced up at her curiously. "For Mura's cries, perhaps."

She shrugged.

"Perhaps, señor, who can say? He will not talk to anyone now except Micaela, the cook, in their Indian language. They keep repeating the word 'nagual.' Do you know what it means, señor?"

"Nagual?" Rennert said. "No, I don't recall ever having heard it."

"I asked the cook what it meant," Madame Fournier seemed worried, "but she said that I must be mistaken, that she had never heard the word."

Rennert asked: "Has the doctor come this morning?"

"No, señor, not this morning, but soon, I think."

Madame Fournier glanced in the direction of the kitchen door, where the girl appeared with Rennert's breakfast.

"At last, señor, she comes—the slow one. You will pardon the delay?"

"Of course, madame."

She removed her hand from his chair, patted the side of her hair, and eyed the approaching girl with disapproval.

"The mangoes are not so fresh this morning as usual, but—" her shrug was expressive—"what will you?"

Rennert assured her that everything was satisfactory. He waited until the girl had set the breakfast things upon the table and returned to the kitchen. Then he said: "Yesterday afternoon, when I was talking to you in the sala, you said something that I should like to ask you about."

"Yes?" Her tone expressed nothing.

"It was about Mr. Shaul. You said that he was not liked by the others in the house. Just what did you mean by that?"

Her eyes were fixed now, sharply, upon his face.

"I meant," she said, "just that. Why do you ask, Señor Rennert?"

"Curiosity merely, madame. When one meets such a well known person as Donald Shaul one is always interested in details of his daily life. Why wasn't he liked?"

"I do not know, señor"—he sensed vagueness in her tone—"it was his manner mostly. He was very disagreeable and often said things that—that got under one's skin, as you Americans say. Sarcastic, that is the word."

"Was he disliked by any one person in particular?"

She considered a moment, while her fingers slowly and carefully moved over the beads.

"Señor Rennert thinks me very, very simple," she said at last with slow careful emphasis, "if he thinks that I believe it is curiosity that makes him ask that question."

With a finger tip Rennert marshaled the knife and fork and spoon into position.

"Let us call it curiosity," he said briefly.

"Very well"—she drew herself up and laughed slightly—"but you might do better to take me into your confidence, Señor Rennert."

"Now, now, madame,"—Rennert glanced up at her and smiled—"you are forgetting that I am here merely on a vacation and that I have no real interest in these people."

"You knew this young man who came yesterday, did you not?" she asked, her eyes belying her casualness of voice.

"I met him on the train, that was all."

"He came to Taxco to see this Miss Noon, did he not?"

"I believe that he did. But you have not answered my question. Was Shaul disliked by any one person in particular?"

He heard her draw a long breath.

"No," she said, "there was no one in particular. He was disliked, I think, by them all."

With another twitch at the rebozo she turned and moved heavily toward the kitchen.

Rennert began upon his mango. He thought: *I wonder why she didn't name the person whom she had in mind.*

El Capitán Heriberto Pérez handed the papers back to Rennert and sat even straighter in his chair. His alert black eyes were fixed on the other's face.

"Ah, yes"—his Spanish was the soft tongue of the lowlands
—"an agent of the Treasury Department of the United States
government. Your identification is satisfactory. It is a pleasure
to have you in our town." He paused, and his fingers stole to
his waxed black mustache. "And you are here . . . ?"

"On a vacation," Rennert assured him. "My status here is
entirely unofficial."

"Ah, yes," the other smoothed his mustache with more
assurance and repeated, "ah, yes." He smiled, revealing white
smooth teeth. "And now, what is it that you have to say to me
about this unfortunate affair in which one of your countrymen
is involved?"

"First, what has been done about the case of the man who
died here last night?"

The other shrugged deprecatingly.

"Ah, that! As yet, señor, we have done little. His body was
removed early this morning, but that is all. There has been this
business of the quarantine. We have been so occupied. The
young man who is involved cannot leave this house during the
quarantine. In the meantime we shall make investigations. It
is," he said very carefully, "very unfortunate, this business.
Both the man who died and the other are citizens of the United
States. Yes," he said again, "it is very unfortunate."

"Certain things have happened here," Rennert said, "that to
my mind make it very doubtful that young Riddle is responsible for Shaul's death. I thought that I should call them to your
attention."

Silence followed his words. The Mexican was gazing out the
window at the mountain tops. His eyes had precisely the im-
penetrability of obsidian. Not a muscle of his face moved.

"Very well," he said at last, as if unwillingly, "what is it you
have to say?"

"In the first place, this Shaul seems to have been rather gen-
erally disliked by the people staying in this house. He was
rendered unconscious by the blow upon his head when he
struck the balustrade. He was carried to his room and lay there
for about three hours before he was found dead. He was alive
at eight-thirty, according to Mrs. Giddings, who has been nursing the boy Esteban, and dead at nine-thirty. When I saw the

body, it lay in an undisturbed attitude, with the covers pulled up to the shoulders and the hands underneath. According to Mrs. Giddings, however, the head was not lying upon the same pillow as when she left the room an hour before. Moreover, the extra pillow had been turned over, and upon the under side is a streak of what can be nothing except blood. Someone, it seems clear to me, entered that room after Mrs. Giddings had left, removed the pillow from beneath Shaul's head, and smothered him with it. Before he died the pressure forced the wound in his head to start bleeding again, and some of the blood streaked the pillow. Also, I believe that an examination of the spots on his trachea and larynx will corroborate my suspicions that suffocation was the direct cause of his death."

He paused and drew from his pocket a pack of cigarettes.

"If you care to go with me into the room next to this I can show you the pillow and let you see for yourself."

The Mexican's eyes fixed themselves upon his face.

"Very well," he said, "let us see."

They arose and went into the next room.

"This," Rennert said, approaching the bed, "is the pillow."

Even as he said it, he knew what had happened.

The pillowcase nearest to them was stiffly starched and white and the blue monogram lay uppermost. There was no streak of red upon the surface. He picked up the other one. Its appearance was the same. He laid it down and faced Pérez. The Mexican's eyes had narrowed ever so slightly.

"During the night," Rennert said, "these pillow cases have been removed and others put in their place."

Another of those long, taut silences, while the Mexican regarded the bed with impassive face.

"To conceal," Rennert said, conscious of the pleonasm of his words, "the fact that a murder had been committed."

The Mexican's smile, when it came, was wide and pleasant and his manner suddenly bland. He said:

"It was after nightfall when you saw this pillow, Mr. Rennert?"

"Yes."

"Ah, that accounts for it, then. Under electric lights things do not look as they look in the daylight. Is it not so?"

Rennert checked his reply and forced a laugh. He saw the futility of further argument and reminded himself that interference in an affair that does not concern one is no way to spend a restful vacation.

"Very well," he said. "You will let the matter drop, then?"

A frown crossed the Mexican's forehead.

"But what would you, Señor Rennert?" He spread his hands in a sudden unstudied gesture. "Even if the pillow had been here, I could not take it and point to a streak of blood and say: 'This man was murdered.' And now there is no streak of blood upon the pillow. What would you have me do?"

"Forget it." Rennert said abruptly. "I'm sorry to have caused you this trouble."

The other's manner became conciliatory.

"But we all make these little mistakes, Señor Rennert. All of us. It is a pleasure to have met you. If it were not for this regrettable affair of the quarantine I should invite you to join me in a *copa* at the cantina at the corner. Perhaps, afterwards."

"Very well—afterwards."

They parted upon the balcony, and Rennert gayly whistled "La Cucaracha" as he returned to his room.

He had stood for a few moments at the window, hands in pockets, when there was a knock at his door. He opened it.

Stephen Riddle stood upon the balcony.

# CHAPTER EIGHT

### CROSS CURRENTS

RIDDLE LOOKED sick. His eyes were bloodshot, with dark pouches beneath them. There was a suspicious tightness about his lips, as if the struggle to retain control of his nerves was concentrated in them. Some of this tightness was in his voice as he spoke.

"Mind if I talk to you a few minutes, Mr. Rennert?"

"Of course not, come in." Rennert stepped aside. "As a

matter of fact," he said as he watched the young man sink heavily into a chair, "I was thinking about you."

"You were?" Riddle said in a flat voice. "Thanks." He seemed at a loss for words.

Rennert extended cigarettes. Riddle took one and accepted a light. His hands moved jerkily.

"In the first place," Rennert said as he sat down, "I'm going to offer some unasked for advice, since you seem to be in a receptive mood. I'd try to get some sleep today, and—I'd let the bottle alone until this affair is over."

Riddle nodded, his eyes half closed.

"Yes, I know. I think I will. I don't hit it this hard—usually. But I've been worried—and now Shaul's death has made things worse." His eyes were very youthful now, and frightened, staring at Rennert. "I didn't mean to kill him. Really—honest to God—no matter what I said to you on the train. I just meant to give him a good beating."

"You think, then, that you did kill him?" Rennert was staring thoughtfully into the smoke which arose in slow spirals from his cigarette.

Riddle's hand paused halfway to his mouth.

"Why, yes, in a way, I did. I hit him, you know, and he fell against the balustrade. They'll hold me responsible." He drew avidly upon the cigarette. "I came up here to ask you what you thought they'd do about it. A Mexican officer talked to me this morning, but I couldn't make out much that he was saying. I haven't sent word to my father yet. I thought I'd wait and see what you said, since you've been down in this country before. I was about ready last night to try and get back to the United States."

Rennert's face grew serious.

"Since you have asked my advice, Riddle, I'll tell you that such a course would be decidedly foolish. This house is under quarantine and is being guarded. Besides, you are being watched. You would never get away, and it would only make your case look worse to the authorities."

Riddle nodded.

"That's what Crenshaw said this morning."

"You know Crenshaw?" Rennert watched his face.

"Not very well. I met him last night down in a bar. He introduced himself and said that he had seen me here in this house. I saw him again this morning at breakfast."

Rennert looked at him thoughtfully.

"If you will wait here a day or two," he said, "there is a good chance that your part in the affair may prove to be a minor one."

With a grimace of distaste Riddle tossed his cigarette, half smoked, through the open window.

"What do you mean?"

"I mean that I am not sure that you *did* kill Shaul." Rennert told him of the discovery of the pillow and of its disappearance during the night. He said nothing of Gwendolyn Noon's visit to Shaul's room.

Riddle listened, his gaze riveted upon Rennert's face. Visibly a tenseness came over his body, and he gripped the arms of the chair until the tendons of his hand stood out stark white against the skin. The muscles about his eyes twitched, and into his eyes came again that dazed look which had been in them when Shaul had lain senseless upon the terrace.

"When did Shaul die?" he demanded thickly.

"Between eight-thirty, when Mrs. Giddings left him, and nine-thirty, when she returned to his room."

Riddle sat staring straight in front of him.

"Do you suspect anyone in particular?" he asked in a low, almost inaudible voice.

"It might have been," Rennert spoke deliberately, "anyone in this house."

"Yes—" the young man hesitated—"it might have been anyone in this house." Rennert, watching him closely, saw the dazed look change slowly into a calculative one.

"Of course," he said, "you will be asked to account for your movements after the time you struck Shaul. You can do that, I suppose?"

"Oh, yes," Riddle spoke abstractedly, "I can do that. I walked down to the plaza after I left you in the dining room. I wanted to cool off a bit and to think things over. I went into a bar and had a few drinks. I was in there when Crenshaw came in and introduced himself. We came back together—you saw us—and

I went up to my room. That must have been a few minutes
after nine, wasn't it?"

Rennert nodded and looked into his bloodshot eyes.

"You went to bed immediately after I saw you go into the
house?"

Riddle averted his eyes. "Yes."

"And you did not leave your room afterwards?" Rennert
leaned forward to crush out his cigarette.

There was a moment's pause.

"No." Riddle's eyes were following the movements of Rennert's fingers.

"Are you sure, Riddle?" Rennert's voice was a probe. "Remember that you asked me to help you in this affair."

He could see the slow, careful narrowing of the averted eyes.
It took away from Riddle's face a great deal of its youthfulness
and left in its place something distinctly less pleasant, something crafty.

"Why do you think I left my room?" he countered, glancing
up quickly at Rennert.

"The doctor who was in the house last night says that he
saw you come up the stairs to this wing after your return with
Crenshaw. He did not see you come down."

Riddle's fingers tightened again about the arms of the chair.

"That's right," he said, "I'd forgotten. I was just walking
around," he faltered, "I wanted to clear my head before I went
to bed."

Rennert got to his feet.

"Sorry, Riddle," he spoke incisively, "it won't do. I should
have been glad to help you out, but I have neither time nor
patience to waste on an exhibition of heroics."

Riddle flinched and a little color suffused his face.

"What do you mean?" he demanded.

"I mean," Rennert had turned his back and was looking out
the window, "that your chivalrous attempt to shield her is
doing Miss Noon's cause more harm than good."

"You think," Riddle got unsteadily to his feet and stared at
Rennert's back, "that I'm trying to shield her?"

"Of course," Rennert wheeled about and faced him. "Aren't
you?"

Riddle's face went white.

"Yes," he said defiantly, "I am. She didn't kill Shaul, and there's no need in her getting mixed up in any investigation. There's bound to be some explanation."

"For what?"

Riddle stared at him for a moment, then jammed his hands into his pockets and raised his chin. There was something histrionic about his defiance now.

"For her not being in her room when I went there last night," he said.

Rennert's face took on a careful lack of expression.

"What time did you go there?"

"About a quarter of an hour, I suppose, after I came back to the house with Crenshaw."

"Don't you think you had better tell me about it?"

"That's all there is to tell." Some of the defiance had gone from Riddle's voice now. "I waited until Crenshaw had gone to his room and everything seemed quiet about the house, then went across to Gwen's—Miss Noon's room. She wasn't there."

"She may have been asleep?"

"No, I knocked; then, when she didn't answer, I opened the door and looked in. The light was on, but she wasn't there."

"You waited?"

"No, I went right back to my room. It would look—well, rather bad for her if anyone saw me there. I just wanted her to go down on the terrace with me and let me talk with her."

"Did you leave your room again during the night?"

"Yes. I went to bed, but I couldn't sleep. The room seemed close and hot, and my head ached. I took another drink or two, then went out on the balcony for a while and smoked. I don't have any idea what time it was."

Rennert remembered the glowing cigarette which he had seen upon the east balcony as Miss Noon had left him at the threshold of Shaul's room. He asked: "How long did you stand on the balcony?"

Riddle shook his head.

"Just long enough to smoke a cigarette. Maybe ten minutes."

Rennert thought a moment. The probable time-schedule of the events of the night seemed clear, as far as Riddle and Miss

Noon were concerned. The young man had returned about nine, had gone to the woman's room at approximately nine-fifteen (his testimony agreed with that of the doctor on this point). At eleven he had been standing upon the balcony and had seen her emerge from Shaul's room; hence his attempt to shield her. But, Rennert wondered, *did* Riddle really believe her guilty? He was inclined to believe that he did, perhaps for more reasons than the apparent ones.

Very deliberately, watching Riddle's face, he said: "You saw, I suppose, who came out of Shaul's room while you were standing on the balcony smoking?"

Riddle stared at him for a moment, as if in surprise.

"Why, yes, I did." His eyes slowly narrowed as he lowered them to the floor. When he looked up they were unnaturally bright. "That accounts, then, for the change of the pillowcases during the night? I had forgotten all about that." There was a trace of relief in his voice which puzzled Rennert.

"Not necessarily," he answered. "In fact, I doubt very much whether it does account for it. I was talking with her in Shaul's room and did not actually see the pillowcase, although she may have had it concealed. I neglected to notice the bed carefully."

"But *I* saw the pillowcase!" Riddle's eagerness was increasing. "She was carrying it when she walked along the balcony toward the stairs. She had it wadded up in her hand, but I'm sure that's what it was."

Rennert regarded him thoughtfully. The obvious desire to incriminate Miss Noon, in such sudden contrast to the previous attempt to protect her, was more and more puzzling. Was it possible that Riddle's earlier attitude had been assumed in order to lend an aspect of truthfulness to this? He might, he admitted, be overestimating Riddle's naïveté.

Before he could speak again there was a sharp rap at the door. He got up, an eye on Riddle's fingers nervously adjusting his tie, and opened it. Crenshaw stood upon the balcony, his large body almost blocking out the sunlight.

"Good-morning," Rennert greeted him.

"Good-morning," was the perfunctory reply. "Is Riddle in your room?"

"Yes," Rennert said, "won't you come in?"

"No," the other answered; "just tell him I'd like to see him right away."

Rennert was observing the man whose features he had been able to discern but indistinctly in the garden the night before. Crenshaw was a tall, strongly built man, probably in his middle forties. His unobtrusive blue serge suit showed signs of wear. He was clean-shaven and had undistinguished, rather homely features: a square prognathous jaw; hard pale-blue eyes that Rennert felt were scrutinizing him as closely as he was their owner; sparse light-brown hair that lay flat upon his head. In some vague manner the man seemed familiar.

"Oh, hello, Crenshaw," Riddle called from inside, "I'll be with you right away."

Riddle passed Rennert at the door. For an instant their eyes met.

"I'll talk to you later in the day," Riddle said. "And—" he swallowed—"thanks a lot."

Rennert closed the door and stood for a long time at the window, staring thoughtfully across the red roofs of Taxco.

Shortly after one o'clock that afternoon Madame Fournier knocked at Riddle's door. The young man had not appeared for luncheon, and Madame, who seemed to be seeking to compensate her guests for their enforced stay by extreme solicitude for their welfare, had explained to María that she was going to find out if he wished a tray brought to him. When no answer came to her repeated knockings, she opened the door and peered into the room.

Riddle lay at full length upon the bed. His coat, vest, and tie had been removed and thrown upon a chair.

Madame Fournier started to close the door; then, as she explained volubly later, struck by a certain unnatural rigidity about his posture, approached the bed. She leaned over and shook Riddle by the shoulder. Riddle was dead.

# CHAPTER NINE

## YELLOW FLOWERS

Rennert stood at the window and stared from beneath comfortably lowered lids into the mountains. A thin, opaque haze cloaked the peaks, dimming perspectives, and nearer at hand there was a hot, unnatural intensity about the sunlight that rendered more mirage-like than ever the pastel backdrop of Taxco. The sky was cloudless and hot blue, pregnant with no promise of the long-delayed rains.

He did not remember ever having experienced a feeling of uneasy tension such as possessed him then. He wondered whether his headache were the cause or the effect. His head throbbed with a dull ache that, as the minutes dragged on, became concentrated at the nape of his neck, where it remained, pressing relentlessly.

As he found himself about to light one cigarette from the end of another, he realized suddenly the reason for the tensity that drew upon his nerves. He was attuned, by the subtle interworkings of man and nature, to the primitive Mexico about him—to the opened fallow fields between the hills, the palmetto-thatched roofs, the drying dust-brown rivers—all in slow-pulsing expectancy, gazing up at the cloudless sky. And waiting. Perhaps, he thought as he virtuously put away the unlighted cigarette, there was something, too, about that house perched on the hillside and the little group of people under its red tiles that contributed to his feeling. He realized now what he had been doing subconsciously all morning. Waiting —just as the land was waiting for the rains. He thought of the house as a stage, set against that pastel backdrop, whereupon they were waiting for the next scene of some imperfectly rehearsed drama.

Rennert carefully and not without some inner regret avoided premonitions. They had no place in his prosaic calling, he always told himself severely. Yet he was to speculate afterwards on what the outcome of those days at Madame Fournier's house might have been had he not deliberately stifled an inner prompting that morning. He might then have understood sooner the

true significance of one of the incidents which preceded the
discovery of young Riddle's body—an incident that presaged
so surely the pitiful epidemic of self-destruction which terrified
the foreign population of Taxco that spring and, because of the
ingenuity of a Mexico City newspaper correspondent alert to
the possibilities of the situation, cast an effective blight upon
the town's tourist trade.

That the victims were Americans was, it developed later,
merely a coincidence due to the fact that these formed by far
the larger part of Taxco's foreign element. But for a time
it seemed that some inexplicable force, emanating from the
centuries-old soil of Mexico, was directing itself or being directed by some unknown agency against the citizens of the Northern Republic. Rennert, confined with that ill-assorted group in
Madame Fournier's house, might have realized the true hid-
eousness of the situation, the long hours of anguish that must
have preceded each of these deaths, but he would have been
helpless to prevent them. Not until the death of Esteban, so
curiously simultaneous with the belated arrival of the rains,
was he able to expose the basis for the superstitious fears that
had been evoked. (And reality, he always said afterwards, was
far more terrible than the worst of the fears of the imagina-
tive.) But even then he could do nothing more.

He was still standing there at the window, staring down at
Taxco's roofs, when in the stillness which lay upon the house
he heard very distinctly the slap of bare feet, like tiny padded
hands, upon the tiles outside his room. They moved past his
door without stopping. He listened for a moment, then walked
to his door and stepped out upon the balcony. There was no
one in sight, but the door of Shaul's room stood ajar. He approached it softly and looked in.

An aged Mexican woman stood by the dresser, her back to
him. She wore a dingy one-piece dress, and about her stooped
shoulders the inevitable rebozo. It slipped slightly, she raised
one hand to adjust it, and Rennert saw what she had been
doing.

Upon the dresser stood the Puebla jar of *talavera* workman-
ship. But the pink and red carnations which it had held the
night before lay now in the fiber basket under the window. In

their stead was a mass of yellow wallflowers that, reflected by the glass of the mirror, seemed to fill that corner of the room with color.

The woman turned her head with a quick, birdlike movement, saw Rennert, and was still. It was not that defensive tautening of the muscles which with other races follows a sudden start and precedes the relaxation of posture. It was rather as if he were looking at a figure of time-worn wax which by some optical delusion had seemed a moment before to have movement. Her face was so corrugated with wrinkles that it might have been a warped Aztec mask fastened to the motionless figure. Only her embedded eyes were vital—black and shrewd and cunning as they ferreted into his.

Rennert stepped into the room.

"*Buenos días,*" he essayed, smiling.

"*Buenos días, señor,*" her voice was slightly staccato yet carried an undertone of soft plaintiveness.

"You are Micaela, the cook, no?" Rennert had neared the jar and was gazing at the golden yellow petals. The atmosphere was heavy with their sweetly pungent odor.

"*Sí, señor,*" one hand began now to stroke very gently the folds of her dress.

"You came to arrange the flowers?"

"*Sí, señor,* I have been so occupied this morning that I could not earlier."

"They are the flowers of death, are they not?"

"*Sí, señor, como no.*" Her voice was patient as if explaining something to a child. "*Son las flores de los muertos.* One has died in this room. I put here yellow flowers."

"You have come before to this, the room of the Señor who has died?"

Even her eyes now lost some of their vitality and were all at once remote.

"No, señor, this is the first time. My work is downstairs." She moved toward the door. "*Con permiso, señor.*"

Rennert stood and watched her go, then looked again at the yellow flowers. He smiled grimly. A characteristic Mexican touch, the association of beauty with death. What are pure-white lilies compared with these savage blossoms that recall, not the futility of the grave, but the sensuous joy of life?

The room in which he stood looked singularly barren now by contrast with these flowers, although as far as he could tell nothing had been removed from it. Nothing, that is, except the body which had lain upon the bed the night before. Rennert whistled softly to himself as he let his gaze wander purposefully about him. He thought: *If the unwilling dead could return, what little objects would they remove from their former habitations and destroy? Odds and ends that betray unguessed-at secrets, frustrations, weaknesses. If they had awareness, these dead, what would be their rage at seeing their privacies invaded!*

He began with the little desk against the north wall. Upon a drop-leaf in the center stood a portable typewriter, and beside it a stack of yellow copy paper. Upon the top was a writing set of Puebla onyx—inkstand, pen, and paper-knife. At the right side, extending to the floor, were three drawers. They proved to be unlocked, and one of them, the lower, was half open. Rennert sat down in the wooden chair and went through their contents carefully.

The two upper drawers contained nothing except a letter addressed to Shaul and more copy paper. The letter, Rennert found when he opened it, was a brief acknowledgment from a publisher of the receipt of a manuscript. Rennert replaced it and bent forward to look more closely at the lower drawer. The woodwork was dented and scarred where it had been forced open. Rennert took the paper-knife from the top of the desk and examined it. He put it back, satisfied that Gwendolyn Noon had used it to open the drawer the night before. He pulled the drawer out to its fullest extent. It was, as he had expected, empty. He stared at the bare board at the bottom, wondering just what papers the woman had abstracted therefrom and burned in the Oaxaca urn. A little wearily he catalogued them mentally and ended with love letters. He closed the drawer and was about to get to his feet when he caught sight of the onyx-backed blotting pad upon the floor. He stooped over and picked it up. He turned it over and held it in the palm of his hand, staring at it thoughtfully.

The blotting paper had been removed from the pad. It looked as if it had been cut away carefully at the ends.

He replaced it upon the top of the desk, then began his search anew. He even thumbed through the blank sheets of copy paper before he gave it up.

He got up and let his eyes travel about the room. He went to the dresser and methodically examined its drawers. They yielded nothing of interest. Shaul's linen had been, his practised eye saw, of an expensive quality. He went to the closet and ransacked the pockets of the two suits and of the overcoat which hung there.

He began next upon the wardrobe trunk which stood beside the bed. It contained, he found, as his search progressed, a carton of American cigarettes, a guest card to a Mexico City club, a Spanish-English dictionary, and three dress collars. In the bottom drawer lay two sheets of copy paper covered with an almost illegible pencil scrawl. Rennert glanced through them with interest, then carried them to the center of the room and sat down in the chair. He lit a cigarette and carefully and thoughtfully read the uneven lines. They were written in an obviously unsteady hand and ran:

> "The house stands on the hillside. . . . It looks like one of those fantastic painted houses on the postcards that one buys on La Avenida Madero to send back home. . . . Mexico, the land of beauty. . . . There is something evil in too much beauty . . . Puritans have always realized that . . . goodness has to be plain . . . my lungs are full of gentleness . . . I look at what comes from my mouth but I see nothing. . . . But up yonder is the house. . . . It is suspended now crazily in midair. . . . But there is no air . . . only emptiness like the emptiness that fills me . . . of course water would bring back life and pulsing red blood . . . but there is no water. . . . The old fellow with the bent leg is singing out under the laurel trees . . . *'Jesu Cristo se ha perdido,'* he is singing . . . Christ himself got lost . . . *'Su madre lo anda buscando'* . . . And his mother is looking for him' . . . *'Caminemos, caminemos, hasta llegar al Calvario, y por más que caminemos, ya lo habrán crucificado.'* . . . And no matter how fast we go to Calvary, she says, they will have Him crucified. . . . Then why hasten, or is the

point of life in the futile hastening? . . . There's something noxious about that house on the hill. . . . I live
there . . . my room has windows that look out on mountains. . . . Yet I am afraid in that house. . . . It is evil
those windows in the sala are two dark eyes watching
me as I sit there. . . . I fill my lungs with smoke again
and look at the house. . . . I run my hand over its red-
tiled roof. . . . The tiles are soft and dry to the touch, for
the rains haven't come yet. . . . Night will be here soon
—it is the night that I fear. . . . Not the night so much
as three o'clock in the morning when everyone is asleep
and I can't sleep . . . and lately there haven't even been
any stars in the sky to look at . . . the rainy season must
be coming soon. . . . Three A. M. and no one awake
except myself and that damned cat that screams and
screams like I'd like to scream and could scream. . . .
They say that animals can sense death in the air. . . .
If that is so, someone is going to die up there on the
hillside—sure as hell. . . . Strange, the feeling I've had
lately as I lie awake at that ungodly hour of the morning
—that someone was standing outside my door. . . . Just
standing there on the balcony and waiting . . . and I lie
there and wait for him to knock but he never does. . . .
Last night I even thought I could hear the sound of low
breathing on the other side of the door. . . . I got up and
tiptoed to the door and threw it open suddenly. . . .
There was no one there. . . . I am going nuts if it keeps
up much longer. . . . Maybe I had better ease up the
pressure there at the house. . . . I surprised a look in
those eyes today—a look that made me almost afraid. . . .
Strange the way this stuff gets your knees and your elbows.
. . . those are the vulnerable places in a man's body . . .
not the head or the lungs or the stomach. . . . I wonder
if I'm crying . . . something I haven't done since I was a
kid and saw that cat that belonged to the little girls next
door run over by a street car . . . damn poor sentence
that . . . I didn't cry because the girl cried or because the
cat was dead . . . she had too many freckles, and the cat
was thin and ugly . . . it was the blood . . . the blood was

so dark and cold when I felt of it. . . . Wonder why I did
that? . . . I always thought blood was hot and red. . . .
There's something that strikes me as funny . . . but I
can't think what it is . . . something like when you've
been drinking whisky all night and talking breathlessly,
without a stop, and all of a sudden it's daylight. . . .
You're surprised and afraid because you've let go of your
moorings—time and duties and hours of sleep and such
things—they've gone . . . and you clutch at the moorings
again desperately to save yourself from the yourself that
you have suddenly come to know . . . the cigarette is
gone—it burned my fingers—and I've thrown it away . . .
and up the hill are cobblestoned streets and stone steps
. . . the Señora at the bar has been watching for the
cigarette to fall from my fingers . . . she says that the
lights will be turned out soon . . . it will be dark then.
. . . Don't I want Miguel to walk with me up the hill to
the house, to the house where the cat is screaming . . .
and someone will be waiting outside my door? . . ."

For a long time Rennert sat there, staring out the window
and holding the two sheets of paper gripped between his
fingers. The odor of the yellow flowers was almost sickening
sweet in his nostrils. He thought: *It was no imagining of
Shaul's that there was a presence upon the balcony. It was
Death who stood there, waiting, and last night knocked at
his door.*

Very carefully he folded the papers and put them into his
pocket. He got up and stepped from the room into the reassur-
ing light and warmth of Taxco's sunshine. He stood for a
moment upon the balcony, undecided, then walked to Mrs.
Giddings's door. He rapped lightly and, when there was no
response, descended the stairs to the sala.

Dr. Parkyn was on the terrace, pacing back and forth in
front of the door. He was, Rennert saw now, a slender man,
evidently strongly built and wiry. He had thick brown hair
with a distinct reddish tinge that was emphasized by the pain-
fully bright sunlight. His features were sharp, astute, and
cruel. As he turned in front of the doorway he caught sight

of Rennert and made a gesture of greeting with his pipe.

"Good-morning, Mr. Rennert."

Rennert stepped upon the terrace.

Parkyn seemed abstracted and continued his pacing.

"Good-morning," Rennert said. "I'm looking for some as-pirin. A headache. You don't have any, by any chance?"

Parkyn paused and looked at him. His clear blue eyes, set closely together, stared through the gold spectacles.

"Aspirin?" he repeated. "No, I don't have any." A smile twisted the corners of his mouth beneath the close-cropped mustache. "Everybody seems to be looking for aspirin this morning. Must be the effect of this weather. I was down trying to talk to that soldier a while ago. He says we're having this unpleasant heat because the rains are late."

Rennert glanced down at the stone steps which led upward to the terrace. At their junction with the cobblestoned street stood a Mexican soldier, his body stiffly erect, yet giving in its ill-fitting uniform a curiously scarecrow effect. Before him, and, it appeared, engaged in animated argument with him, was a woman. She was, he could tell at a glance, an American. Middle-aged, dressed plainly, yet with a touch of the incongruous—high-heeled, polished oxfords that were never meant for Taxco's cobblestones, an enormous silver bracelet upon a thin bony wrist, a multicolored fibre handbag—that stamped her unmistakably as one of that unself-conscious, self-assertive group which has invaded Mexico in such numbers in recent years. As Rennert watched, her resistance seemed to collapse before the Indian stolidity of the soldier—as, the Mexicans say, all newcomers to Mexican soil must collapse at last before its immutability. As she turned away she glanced up at the house, so that Rennert caught a glimpse of her face. It was tight and drawn and looked, in the intense sunlight, singularly lifeless. She stared at the house for a moment, then drew a hand across her eyes with a slow uncertain gesture. There was something stiff and unnatural about her slow progress over the cobblestones toward the Little Street of the Hidden Waters.

"Have you been vaccinated for the smallpox?" Parkyn asked.

"Yes—" Rennert rested a foot upon the balustrade and

looked down the hillside—"a commonsense precaution before coming to Mexico—or any place else."

"I have too," Parkyn said. "I was just thinking that we had better be sure everybody in the house has been—" he stared into the bowl of his pipe and said matter-of-factly—"just in case Esteban's illness *should* prove to be the smallpox."

"I supposed," Rennert said, "that the doctor would see to that, but it might be well to remind the guests here." He looked down at the tiles for a moment thoughtfully. "By the way," he said, "I understand that Esteban has been repeating something like 'nagual' since he was told that it was Madame Fournier's cat which was doing the screaming. I wondered if you knew what the word meant."

Parklyn stared at him, his eyes drawn into a squint.

"Nagual?" he repeated gutterally. "Are you sure?"

"According to Madame. The cook, however, told her that she must be mistaken, that she had never heard the word."

"The cook is an Indian too, isn't she?"

"Yes."

Parkyn nervously adjusted his spectacles upon his nose so that his eyes lost some of the squinting effect.

"Interesting," he said and repeated, "interesting. I'll have to talk to the boy and find out whether that's what he really said." He glanced at his watch. "I have an engagement now. I'll see you later in the day, probably." He thrust his pipe into the left side of his mouth, gripped it with his teeth and said: "Such a survival is entirely possible in a country like Mexico."

# CHAPTER TEN

### THE CAT SCREAMS AGAIN

A THIN WISP of blue smoke trailed serpentine-like in Parkyn's wake as he walked with his queer ambling gait into the sala and toward the stairs. Rennert watched the smoke dissolve in the hot still air, then decided to try some lunch and a cup of black Mexican coffee. The scientist's recognition of the word "nagual" worried him. Probably, he told himself as he crossed the sala, because it injected a new and unpredictable element into an already complicated affair.

The dining room was cool and smelled faintly damp, despite the warm air that entered through the open windows.

Mandarich and Crenshaw were seated at a table by a window. Mandarich was talking excitedly, gesturing with his hands. He hailed Rennert as the latter entered.

"We've been talking," he said as Rennert sat down at their table, "about the possibility of doing something about this quarantine business. It's nonsense that we should be cooped up here like this. Both Mr. Crenshaw and I, and I daresay all this crowd, have been vaccinated for smallpox, and most of us have probably had the measles. We're all citizens of the United States, and it seems to me that our ambassador in Mexico City ought to do something about it." He paused and eyed his companion as if for support.

Crenshaw raised his eyes from contemplation of his cigar and fixed them on Rennert.

"A Mexican officer was asking this morning where your room was located. I thought that you might have some information about how long this quarantine is likely to last." He was freshly shaved, and his face looked pink and healthy, with particles of talcum powder visible beneath the lobes of the ears.

"Frankly," Rennert said, "I don't know. The regular doctor is expected back from Mexico City tomorrow or the day after, and he may be able to diagnose the boy's case better than his assistant. I understand that he isn't sure whether it is measles or smallpox. I think that the authorities are waiting until he returns."

"Then you're willing to sit around here and wait?" Mandarich broke a French roll with petulant emphasis.

Rennert smiled and watched the artist's fingers crumbling the bread over the tablecloth.

"I came down here for a vacation," he said. "I'm afraid that several days of enforced inactivity rather appeal to me."

"Your visitor evidently didn't give you much information, then." Crenshaw continued to regard Rennert. It was not a

stare so much as a steady unhurried appraisal. Rennert realized
that under certain circumstances it might be disconcerting.

"No, he didn't," he said.

"*Qué desea tomar, señor?*" the little Indian waitress said
softly at his side.

Rennert surveyed the menu and gave his order. The girl
nodded and disappeared quickly into the kitchen.

"Did he," Crenshaw asked evenly, "say anything about
young Riddle's case?"

"Very little, except that it was unfortunate and that investigations would be made."

"What do you think they're likely to do about it—hold him
for manslaughter?"

"Probably," Rennert said carefully. "The situation is likely
to prove very awkward for Riddle, although the popular conception of the mistreatment of Americans who get entangled
with the Mexican law is an exaggerated one. I should say
that he will fare as well, if not better, than if the same thing
had happened in the United States."

"He will be allowed to stay here in the house during the
quarantine, won't he?"

"Yes, I'm sure."

With a short blunt forefinger, Crenshaw carefully broke the
ash of his cigar over his plate.

"By that time," he said, "the American Embassy in Mexico
City should have gotten busy."

"They have been notified?" Some of his surprise was in
Rennert's voice.

"Yes, I arranged with the officer in charge here to send word
to them this morning, as soon as I heard of Shaul's death."

The waitress was placing a steaming bowl of soup before
Rennert.

"You knew Riddle before he came to Taxco, then?" he
remarked to Crenshaw with, he felt, unconvincing casualness.

"No." Crenshaw's eyes met his. "I never saw him before
last night."

For a moment their eyes held. Rennert was increasingly
certain that what he read in Crenshaw's steady gaze was a

challenge. *Maybe,* he thought, *he has abrogated to himself—
as I have—the rôle of detective in this tangle. . . .*

It was at this moment that the Siamese cat screamed.

Even Crenshaw's eyes went for an instant to the doorway
of the sala, whence the sound had proceeded. The lacquer tray
fell from the hands of the waitress and struck the floor with
a clatter.

Rennert glanced at her. She was standing, her hands twisting and untwisting. Her brown oval face was impassive, but
her dark eyes glinted with fear.

"Do not have fear," he spoke to her quietly, "it is the cat,
nothing else."

"*Sí, señor,*" she murmured picking up the tray, "that is
what they say."

She started to walk toward the kitchen door but, halfway
there, broke into a run. Rennert watched the door swing to
behind her, then found himself again looking into Crenshaw's
eyes.

"Ah, that cat!" Mandarich drained a glass of water ."She
makes me nervous when she screams like that. Someone should
get rid of her."

His face was round and bland, in curious contrast with the
tremor that edged his voice.

"This morning," Crenshaw said quietly, "someone very
nearly did."

"Yes?" Mandarich swallowed quickly. "How was that?"

Crenshaw tapped his cigar gently upon the side of his plate.

"Rat poison," he said in his clipped speech.

"Rat poison?" Mandarich put down his glass and stared at
Crenshaw. His half-opened mouth gave his face an almost
stupid appearance.

"Yes. Old lady Fournier had some out in the kitchen. She
missed it and found that it had been put into the cat's food.
It was in some mashed-up tortillas, though, and the cat
wouldn't eat it. The old lady raised hell and is trying to find
out who did it. She thinks——"

He broke off and looked straight in front of him. He got up
from his chair.

Rennert, turning, saw the object of his gaze.

Madame Fournier was standing in the doorway, one hand resting upon the jamb as if for support. Her face was haggard, and in her eyes Rennert read an old woman's weariness, a weariness of life and all that it entailed.

"Upstairs," she said in a tight choking voice, "in his room. He is dead."

"Who?" Crenshaw strode toward her.

"The young man who came yesterday. Mr. Riddle." She gestured upwards.

Crenshaw had passed her and was taking the stairs to the east wing three at a time. Rennert followed him a little more slowly.

The door of Riddle's room stood open. When Rennert entered Crenshaw was beside the bed, leaning over Riddle's body. He straightened up and glanced quickly about the room. His gaze came to rest upon the table beside the bed. Upon its surface stood an empty glass and a small pasteboard box, unlabeled. It was half open and disclosed a few small white tablets.

There was a purposive glitter in Crenshaw's cold blue eyes as he picked up the box and extracted one of the tablets. His jaw seemed to be thrust forward at a more than usually belligerent angle as he examined it. His eyes went slowly to the white set face upon the bed, and a slowly calculative look came into them. He replaced the box upon the table and turned to Rennert.

"Stay here," he said curtly, "while I call the doctor."

Rennert's face was expressionless as he watched him walk from the room. Then he went to the table and took one of the tablets from the box. He applied it to the tip of his tongue. It was, he knew at once, veronal. He stared for a moment thoughtfully at the bed.

Freckles were evident now on Riddle's face, whitened and with its features sharpened into pale asceticism by the curious pinched pallor of death. Suddenly his eyes narrowed, and he bent over the right hand which lay outstretched on top of the sheet, beside Riddle's body. Across the back were five scratches, their edges distended by dried blood. Rennert stared at them, a frown on his face.

He began to walk slowly about the room, his hands thrust deep into his pockets. Riddle had not yet unpacked his belongings. One suitcase lay open upon a rack, another stood on the floor beneath the window. A soiled shirt lay beside it. And beyond, in the corner, two crumpled white cloths. Rennert picked them up. They were soiled pillowcases. Upon one side of each was a small "F" monogrammed in blue thread. On the surface of one was a faint yet unmistakable streak of brown.

He held them in his hands for a moment, his thoughts busy, then laid them on the table.

The Mexican soldier walked quickly into the room, followed by Crenshaw. The Mexican's excitement was manifest in his gait and in the way his eyes flicked Rennert's face in a sideways glance as he approached the bed. Rennert saw Crenshaw's eyes fasten themselves almost immediately upon the pillowcases.

"Where'd they come from?" he demanded, his fingers toying with a broken match.

"They are pillowcases which I found upon the floor," Rennert replied briefly. To the soldier he said: "I found these upon the floor of this room. I think that el Capitán Pérez will be interested in them. Will you do me the favor of giving them to him?"

The Mexican glanced inquiringly and a little suspiciously at Rennert, took the cases, and folded them with careful fingers.

"Sí, señor," he acquiesced.

Rennert nodded to him and turned toward the door.

"I shall be in my room," he said, "if el Capitán wishes to speak to me." Crenshaw, he saw, was staring at him, the match gripped between his white, even teeth.

"Sí, señor, como no." The soldier seemed undecided whether or not to oppose his departure.

Rennert saw Crenshaw's cold blue stare directed against his face as he left the room and stepped out upon the balcony. He was not surprised when, half-way to the stairs, he was halted by a cold even voice that held a trace of peremptoriness: "Rennert!"

He turned and regarded the man who was advancing toward him.

Crenshaw held his head lowered a trifle and his hands, held

at his sides, had their fingers turned slightly inwards, so that he gave the impression of a wrestler about to spring. His face was hard and impassive and talcum-sprinkled. He came to a stop before Rennert and thrust his hands into his pockets as if he were putting them into a sheath.

"What was the idea," he said without removing the match from his teeth, "of giving those pillowcases to that soldier?"

Rennert met his gaze squarely.

"None, possibly. I merely thought that they ought to be called to the attention of the captain in charge here."

Crenshaw's eyes narrowed slightly, so that they looked like particles of cold glass.

"Is there any reason why a pair of pillowcases upon the floor should be of interest to the police in the case of a suicide?"

"Not necessarily," Rennert replied noncommittally and waited, his eyes still fixed on the man's face.

Crenshaw stepped forward slightly and, jerking the match from his mouth, directed the tip at Rennert.

"See here, Rennert—" his voice hardened and he carefully spaced his words—"I don't know what your game is in this business, though I've got an idea. You're wasting your time, fellow, you're wasting your time. Riddle's dead now, and that's the end of him. Better look for a new racket."

He swiveled about on his heels and strode along the balcony to his room.

Rennert stood and watched his broad back disappear, then walked down the stairs to the sala.

At the foot of the staircase he stood by the bowl of scarlet noche buena flowers and gazed at the dust-filmed top of the table which stood at his left. He went over to it, pushed aside the volume of Tennyson, and opened the ledger. Slowly and thoughtfully he ran his eyes over the names of the guests registered in Madame Fournier's pension.

Mrs. Sarah Giddings, of Indianapolis, Ind., had registered on March 27, almost three months before. Hers was a firm, precise, almost colorless signature. It called to Rennert's mind, somehow, her voice as she had announced to him that Shaul was dead.

Albert Martineau Mandarich, of New York City, had signed his name in a round flowing script on April 11.

Dr. R. L. Parkyn's small, pinched handwriting had been put in the book three weeks before, the last of May. Dr. Parkyn's address was Chicago.

Between the arrival of Dr. Parkyn and that of Gwendolyn Noon, Madame Fournier had evidently purchased a new bottle of ink, for the signature of the actress was in black, in contrast with the watery blue of the three previous names. Miss Noon had registered two weeks before, from New York City.

Two days after her, Donald Shaul had put his signature upon the book. At first Rennert didn't recognize it, this signature of Shaul's, so illegibly was it scrawled across the page.

George Crenshaw, of Dallas, Texas, wrote with a firm hand, pressing down upon the slightly splayed pen point. He had registered the day after Shaul. Rennert noticed that Crenshaw had evidently blotted the paper immediately after signing, for only on the edges was the signature distinct. Between, the pen point had left no mark, so that the letters of his name were etched firmly in white-relieved black.

Stephen Riddle's signature was immediately above Rennert's. It wavered and fell below the horizontal blue line that crossed the page.

Rennert's gaze went back and rested on Mrs. Giddings's signature. He thought: *Her words, her actions, even her writing, are under rigid control. What emotion is she afraid of showing?* He took up the volume of Tennyson's poems which lay beside the ledger and opened it to the place where the sheet of notepaper had been inserted by Madame Fournier. The poem that met his eye was "The Lotos-Eaters." Phrases had been underlined with a hard-leaded pencil.

> "*'Courage!' he said, and pointed toward the land,*
> *'This mounting wave will roll us shoreward soon.'*
> *In the afternoon they came unto a land*
> *In which it seemèd always afternoon.*"

Rennert's gaze went to the tiles of the terrace where sunlight glared. He put the book under his arm and walked across the sala, up the stairs, and to his room. He sat in a chair and read "The Lotos-Eaters." Half-remembered words

and phrases came back to him poignantly, underlined here by
a careful methodical pencil.

"*Dark faces pale against that rosy flame,*
*The mild-eyed melancholy Lotos-eaters came.*"

He started to yawn, a tribute to the soporific melody of the
lines, and walked, with eyelids heavy, to the window.

He stood there for a long time, staring thoughtfully into the
mountains that ring Taxco. Their impersonal remoteness, he
had found, was an unexcelled framework for pasting on
thoughts. And thoughts, he was finding, were difficult to
marshal.

He was still at the window when Captain Pérez knocked
at his door.

The Mexican's face was grave, and his greeting was more
formal than usual. His handshake was perfunctory.

When he had sat down and lighted a cigarette he spoke in
a low tense voice: "Now, Señor Rennert, what does it mean—
the death of this young man? It is suicide, *no es claro?*"

Rennert smoked for a moment in silence.

"That would be the simplest explanation, of course," he said.

The Mexican was regarding him closely, his eyes obsidian.
"But you do not think so?"

"No, I don't." Rennert drew upon his cigarette. "It is too
simple, the explanation that Riddle killed Shaul, then—either
out of remorse or fear of the consequences of his act—committed suicide by taking veronal. And then there are those pillowcases——"

"But yes," the Mexican's murmur was soft, "my man gave
them to me. You think they are the ones which disappeared
from the room of this Shaul last night?"

"Yes, I'm sure of it. We were meant to find them in Riddle's
room and to think that it was he who went to Shaul's room
and removed them."

"It is possible that that is true, is it not?"

"Yes," Rennert admitted, "but why would he bring them to
his room, where they would be sure to be found? Why not
hide them somewhere else about the house? And why—for that
matter—remove them at all? Even if he had known last night
of Mrs. Giddings' suspicions, he would have had nothing to

gain by so doing. On the contrary, it would be to his advantage to leave in Shaul's room the proof that he had been smothered with the pillow. There would be, then, at least the alternate possibility that another person, another enemy of Shaul's, had entered the room. Unless—" he got to his feet and walked slowly toward the window—"he knew last night that he had been seen coming up the stairs to this wing."

"He was seen, then?" A trace of eagerness was in the captain's voice.

"Yes, by Dr. Otero, the young fellow who is taking care of the mozo. It must have been about nine-fifteen when he saw Riddle go up the stairs. Riddle's explanation to me this morning was that he went to Miss Noon's room, at the head of the stairs, that she was not there, and that he returned to his own room in the other wing."

"But where, then, was this Miss Noon?" The Mexican put the question softly.

Rennert stared out the window in silence for a few moments. In clattering cacophony came the sound of a donkey's feet on the cobblestones below. He flipped the end of his cigarette into space and watched it twirl to the rocky ground. He turned and faced Captain Pérez.

"Miss Noon," he said, "has been on my mind ever since the discovery of Riddle's body. If we accept the young man's testimony, suspicion certainly points to her." He told of his encounter with her in Shaul's room the night before. "She undoubtedly was concealing something under her cloak and"—he began to pace restlessly up and down—"Riddle stated definitely that he saw the pillowcases in her hand as she walked down the balcony." He came to an abrupt halt in front of the Mexican, his face suddenly grim, then sat down in the chair and slowly extracted a pack of cigarettes from his pocket. He selected one, lit it, and looked through the smoke into the black eyes opposite him. "Which, of course, was a lie."

"A lie?" Pérez's fingers crept upward to his waxed mustache.

"Yes. Riddle couldn't have seen what she was carrying in her hand. It was past eleven o'clock, and there were no lights on the balcony."

The other slowly caressed the silky black hairs and waited,

like—the irrelevant thought came to Rennert—an animal about
to pounce.

"It would seem," Rennert went on, "that Riddle wished to
incriminate the woman. He told me that she was out of her
room during the period when Shaul was murdered and that
she carried the pillowcases from his room later." Rennert shook
his head slowly. "But I was positive that he really *did* wish to
shield her and that his reluctance to reveal the fact that she
was not in her room when he went there was not feigned. I
still don't think that I was wrong."

"And now," the Mexican commented, "the young man is
dead from an overdose of veronal." He considered a moment.
"He was enamored of her, was he not?"

Rennert nodded. He was thinking: *But, if Noon wished to
get those papers from Shaul, why didn't she get them after
she smothered him, rather than risk a return to his room?*

"Yes," he said, "but she had broken off her engagement
with him."

"Ah!" Pérez grasped this eagerly. "That is the explanation,
is it not? He was angry when she did this and wished to harm
her. Later, when he thought about it, he felt the remorse and
killed himself."

"Leaving however, no refutation of his words to me."

"No, he was probably overwrought and did not think of
them. He may have thought, too, that the circumstances of
his death and the finding of the pillowcases in his room would
be sufficient evidence that he—and not she—was guilty."

Rennert leaned his head against the back of the chair and
stared at the whitewashed ceiling.

"No," he said in a few moments, "that won't do. If I read
Riddle's character right, a more likely explanation would be
that he believed—whether rightly or not doesn't matter—that
she was guilty and took this means of shielding her. He may
have found the pillowcase in her room this morning and considered that it constituted damning proof against her. If it
were not for his words about seeing the pillowcase in her hand
last night, I should be inclined to this theory. That's the point
that bothers me. It doesn't seem to fit. And then there is the
question about the veronal."

"The veronal?"

"Yes. Where did Riddle get it? From what I saw of him I should scarcely think that he was likely to keep a supply of it at hand. And I very much doubt whether one could buy it in any *botica* in Taxco. Then, too, there is the fact that the box is unlabeled. Someone may have given it to him and told him it was something else, something perfectly harmless—aspirin, say."

Silence lay heavy between them for several moments.

"Señor Rennert," Pérez carefully flicked an imaginary speck of dust from the knee of his breeches, "I am going to be frank with you. I fear that you are too suspicious. I understand your wish to see justice done in a matter which concerns your countrymen, but for me the affair is," he gently stressed the words, "very awkward. Many Americans come each year to Taxco, and I am sure that it would be the wish of the authorities to avoid any scandal. I hope that this young man's death will prove to have been a suicide, so that the affair can be closed quickly. But your suspicions about the death of this Mr. Shaul were, it would seem, correct. So I am going to inquire into these matters which you have mentioned. Then, if we learn nothing further to justify your suspicions, we shall call the case closed. This is satisfactory?"

Rennert's smile was frank.

"Of course. As I said before, it is no concern of mine, after all, if the entire American colony here is wiped out. It was through no fault of mine that I have gotten mixed up in this case as much as I have."

Pérez was immediately conciliatory.

"You will understand, of course, Mr. Rennert, that I appreciate deeply your aid. I trust, also, that you will assist me in my investigations."

"Assist you?"

"Yes, my English is," the Captain shrugged, "very little. And you know these people here, their reactions, their customs. You can address your questions to them and tell them that you are acting for me."

"But," Rennert laughed, "I'll be about as welcome as a sore thumb about this house if they find out that you suspect one of them of being a murderer and that I'm helping you in the investigation."

The Captain considered a moment.

"Suppose," he suggested, "that we tell them merely that you are my interpreter."

"Very well," Rennert said. "It looks as if this would prove to be a postman's holiday for me."

"*Bueno,*" the Mexican gently rubbed the palms of his hands together. "Whom shall we interview first?"

"I think," Rennert said, "that Miss Noon may be able to enlighten us on several points."


# CHAPTER ELEVEN

## IN THE AFTERNOON

T HE MEXICAN SOLDIER held the door open for Gwendolyn Noon, bowed slightly when she had entered, and closed it softly.

She paused for a moment, looking at the two men who stood before her. She wore a long-sleeved silk dress whose sheer whiteness made more startling by contrast the sallowness of her complexion and the dark shadows about her eyes. The fingers of her crimson-nailed right hand played nervously with the heavy gold bracelet upon her left wrist.

"Won't you sit down, Miss Noon?" Rennert motioned toward a chair. He was thinking: *I wonder if she purposely wears a long-sleeved dress to conceal that bruise upon her elbow?*

She moved forward uncertainly and sank into the chair. He offered a cigarette. As he extended a match he noticed the trembling of her long white fingers. Their brightly lacquered nails gave them a curiously fragile appearance. When the cigarette was lighted she sank back in the chair and drew upon it with long avid inhalations.

"This," Rennert indicated his companion, "is Captain Pérez, who is investigating the circumstances of Mr. Riddle's death."

He could see the slow tensing of the muscles of her face as she looked at the Mexican and inclined her head. Her eyes came quickly back to Rennert.

"But what's the use?" she asked with a trace of weariness. "He's dead now."

"The Captain speaks little English," Rennert went on, "and has asked me to interpret for him. I think," he lowered his voice and looked at her steadily, "that under the circumstances it will be necessary for you to tell us about those papers which you burned in Shaul's room last night. It was blackmail, wasn't it?"

Her teeth sank into her lower lip, and the muscles about her eyes twitched. After a moment she nodded abstractedly.

"It makes no difference now. You may as well know." She stared into the smoke of her cigarette with eyes which had again a strangely dilated look. "You're right—" she spoke in a low, almost inaudible voice—"Shaul had been blackmailing me. When I learned that he was dead I went to his room to get—what he was threatening me with." She looked up at Rennert. "Isn't that enough?"

"I think," he said evenly, "that it would be better if you told us all about it."

"Very well." Her fingers tightened about the arms of the chair so that the knuckles stood out stark white against the bloodless skin. "He had a copy of my marriage certificate." She leaned back her head and closed her eyes, and let the smoke trickle slowly from her half-open lips. Her voice was recitative. "Years ago, while I was in the chorus of a Broadway show, I married a man—his name doesn't matter. We lived together for a time, then he left me. There was no quarrel, we just got tired of each other. For a while we corresponded occasionally, but for over a year now I haven't heard from him. I never took the trouble to get a divorce, it simply made no difference one way or the other. Then Stephen Riddle came along. He offered me marriage, money, a social position. Press notices hadn't been so good—and I saw the end of my career in sight, so I decided to get out while I could—in a blaze of glory. I want you to understand"—she opened her eyes and straightened up in her chair—"that I really liked Riddle. He was younger than I, of course—he never knew how much younger—but I think I could have made a success of the marriage. He didn't know I had been married before, so I came to Mexico to get my divorce. You guessed that, didn't you?"

"Yes," Rennert said, "it was the only explanation for your trip down here. But why the secrecy as far as Riddle was concerned? I shouldn't have thought that he would raise an objection on account of your previous marriage."

"It was his father." She stared at the cone of ash upon her cigarette. "He's a strict Catholic and would have disowned Stephen if he had married a divorcée. It would have been, from what Stephen told me, hard enough to get him to agree to a marriage with an actress, in any case."

"You met his father?"

"No, I was to marry Stephen as soon as I got back from Mexico, and we were going to trust that his father would accept the marriage when it was over with."

"And when did Shaul appear on the scene?"

"He came down here soon after I did. He may have heard about my proposed marriage with Riddle in New York and followed me down. He had the proof of my former marriage, a copy of the marriage certificate, and threatened to send it to Riddle's father. I had enough money to put him off for a time, but not enough to satisfy him. To force me to get some more, he began to hint at my predicament in his column. Then Stephen came down and," she shrugged, "you know the rest."

"And what was it that you took from Shaul's room last night?" Rennert was studying her face. It had an unnatural rigidity about it that might, he knew, precede a flood of emotions.

"The copy of my marriage certificate. I destroyed it." She leaned toward the table and crushed out the cigarette.

"You took nothing out of the room with you?"

She stared at him, the muscles about her lips beginning to twitch as her fingers continued to crush the tobacco.

"No, nothing else. What else would I want from his room?"

Rennert waited a moment, then said carefully: "Riddle told me that he saw you leave Shaul's room and that you were carrying a pair of pillowcases."

She stared at him dazedly.

"You say Stephen told you that?" she asked in a colorless voice.

"Yes. I remembered afterwards, however, that it was dark upon the balcony when you and I left the room. I wondered how Riddle could have seen you with the cases in your hand."

"But pillowcases?" she asked. "Why should I take pillowcases from his room? I don't understand."

"Because," Rennert said steadily, "those pillowcases constituted proof that Shaul was smothered in his room while unconscious."

"Smothered!" She leaned forward quickly, the last vestige of color gone from her face. "You're sure of that?"

"Yes."

Her eyes left his face, and she stared fixedly at the calla lilies in the shallow bowl upon the table by the window.

"You think Riddle did it?" she asked in a low voice.

"No," Rennert said, "I don't, despite the fact that the pillowcases were found in his room this morning."

"In his room?"

"Yes, after the discovery of the body."

She said, "Oh!" tonelessly and kept staring at the lilies.

"Riddle also told me," Rennert said, "that he knocked at your door last night about nine-fifteen and that you were not there."

"No," she said in the same abstracted tone, "I wasn't. I was down in Madame Fournier's room."

"That was during the interval when Shaul was murdered," Rennert said in the same even tone.

She drew a sharp breath and half arose from her chair, her eyes flashing. There was a slight flush upon her cheeks.

"You think, then, that I did it!" she cried. "You got me to tell about Shaul blackmailing me so as to get a motive. But you're lying about Riddle saying that he saw me with the pillowcase in my hand. He didn't say that! He couldn't have!"

She got to her feet and stood, the nails of her fingers digging into the palms of her hands.

"I'm not to consider myself under arrest, am I?" she demanded in a suddenly calm voice.

"No," Rennert said, "you are not."

"Very well, then, I have nothing more to say."

"Just a moment," Rennert spoke as she turned away, "there is one more question I should like to ask."

She paused, one hand on the door knob.

"Yes?"

"Riddle died from an overdose of veronal. Have you any idea where he could have obtained it?"

Her fingers tightened upon the metal.

"No." There was defiance in her voice.

"You never by any chance gave him any?"

Her eyes were queer, now, and sharp, and he sensed a wariness about her.

"No," she spoke breathlessly, "of course not. I hadn't any to give him."

Rennert studied her face for a moment, then got up and walked to the table, pulled out a drawer, and took from it a clean sheet of notepaper bearing the engraved blue "F" of Madame Fournier's pension. He laid it carefully upon the top of the table, took from his pocket a fountain pen and wrote (after a momentary hesitation) the word "nagual." From the still open drawer he selected one of three sheets of blotting paper and dried the ink. He laid the blotting paper beside the notepaper and turned to the woman.

"Miss Noon," he said pleasantly, "would you be kind enough to look at that paper and see if you recognize the word which I have written."

She stared at him with a puzzled frown, then walked to the table and picked up the paper. She stood for a moment gazing at it before he saw her eyes roving over the table top and the open drawer. When she looked up her breath seemed to be coming faster, and her fingers tightened upon the paper.

"No," she shook her head decidedly, "I never saw it before. What is it—Spanish?" She let the paper fall to the table.

"That is what I have been wondering," Rennert said. "Esteban, the sick boy downstairs, has been repeating it."

She forced a laugh.

"I don't know a half dozen words of Spanish. You'll have

to get somebody else, I'm afraid." She moved toward the door.
"Is there anything else?"

"No, Miss Noon, that is all. And thank you."

She did not turn, but fumbled for a moment with the knob,
opened the door, and went out.

When she had gone Rennert went to the table and wrote
her initials upon the sheet of paper which Gwendolyn Noon
had held. Very carefully he placed it among the pages of the
volume of Tennyson which lay upon the table. He walked
then slowly to the window and stood staring at a gray adobe
wall, half masked by trees, on the hillside below.

"And what," Pérez asked, "did the woman say?"

Rennert turned and laughed. He had forgotten that the Captain had understood none of their conversation. He recounted
it in detail.

Pérez listened, his face imperturbable. For several moments
after Rennert had concluded he said nothing, but sat gently
stroking with one finger the silky hairs of his mustache.

"You believe her?" he asked at last.

"Frankly," Rennert said thoughtfully, "I am not sure whether
I do or not. Part of her testimony I am inclined to believe—
the part about the previous marriage and Shaul's blackmailing.
That fits in with the evidence very well. Also, strange to say,
I have the feeling that she was telling the truth when she pro-
fessed ignorance of the pillowcases. I don't think that she *did*
carry them out of Shaul's room. At least," he amended carefully, "when I was there." He smoked for a moment in silence.
Might she have gone there at an earlier hour of the evening?
he was asking himself. Before the lights were extinguished.
As Riddle stood upon the other balcony he might have seen her
come out of Shaul's room. But in that case, why had he not
followed her to her own room if he wished to talk to her?
And why had she not secured the paper then? An inter-
ruption? . . .

"This Miss Noon is an actress," Pérez reminded Rennert.

"Yes," Rennert nodded slowly, "I have kept that in mind,
as well as the fact that a person in her state is capable of an
extraordinary degree of cunning. It makes her words and actions highly unpredictable." He tapped a cigarette upon the

arm of his chair. "Let us talk now to Madame Fournier and learn if Miss Noon *did* visit her about nine-fifteen."

Pérez nodded acquiescence and went to the door to give the directions to his subordinate on the balcony.

"Why your question about the veronal?" he asked as he sat down again. "You think that she may have given it to the young man?"

"That, I'll admit, was my first thought. She is, as you could probably see at once, a drug addict."

"*Sí.*" From the expressionless monosyllable and the shrug which accompanied it Rennert could not determine whether the Mexican were surprised or not. "That accounts, then, for her manner."

"Yes. I am positive that she uses drugs regularly and that for some reason she is unable to obtain them now. She is growing more and more desperate and has reached the stage where she would be capable of anything in order to satisfy her craving. All along I have had an alternate explanation for her visit to Shaul's room last night—that she went for the copy of the marriage certificate, as she said, but also for drugs."

"He was supplying her with them?" The Mexican was watching Rennert carefully.

"Yes, he was himself a smoker of marihuana, as I know from a paper on which he had written down some of his thoughts while under the influence of the weed. I found it in his trunk this morning."

"Ah!" Pérez leaned forward slightly. "You searched his room, then?"

"Yes." Rennert looked straight into his eyes. "Do you object to my having done so?"

As with a slight effort the Mexican shrugged again.

"Of course not, Señor Rennert. You were saying?"

"She did not find the drug that she was looking for—I could ce that from her manner just now—but it is my theory that ;haul was supplying her with the stuff, that he had been resorting to a common practice among his kind and had been raising the price on her until he was asking more for it than she could pay. In that case she would be frantic."

He was conscious of the directness of the Mexican's gaze.

"If that were true——" the latter began.

There was a light tapping at the door.

"If that were true," Rennert finished grimly, "she may well have murdered him in the hope of getting some more."

He stepped to the door and admitted Madame Fournier.

The old woman seemed to have recovered somewhat from the shock which she had displayed at the discovery of Riddle's body, although her eyes were tired and tear-filled, and her face seemed to have aged incredibly.

"Señores, I am ruined!" she exclaimed in voluble Spanish. "Who will come now to my house? Two men dead and this Esteban on the point of death. And this 'quarantine! There is a curse on this house! It will be as the cook says, on account of that Señor Parkyn! I shall have to——"

"Why on account of Parkyn?" Rennert interrupted.

She sat down and tugged the black rebozo closer about her shoulders.

"It is," she shrugged and averted her eyes, "but another superstition of these *indios,* but—*quién sabe?*—perhaps they know more of these things than we think. *El señor* Parkyn spends his time out in these hills searching for idols and masks —what all I do not know. The cook says that the ancient ones do not like being disturbed. Esteban went with him once, down into la Tierra Caliente—" she gestured vaguely southward— "and when he returned he fell sick. He has not yet gotten out of his bed. It may be an illness which has been sent upon him to punish him." Her fingers were plucking at the fringe of the rebozo. "The cook says that this sickness is the *pinto.* You know what that is, señor?"

"Yes." Rennert nodded. For an instant, almost too brief to be discernible, he had seen something glint in Captain Pérez's eyes, as if a ray of light had glanced against their obsidian blackness. Even as he looked, it was gone. The Captain, he knew, was from the Hot Lands south of Taxco, along the river Balsas, where lurks, according to popular superstition, that dread disease known vaguely as "the pinto"—the discolor.

"But Parkyn did not fall sick," Rennert reminded the woman.

"Not yet, señor," she was fingering her beads now, "but he may be the next, who knows?"

In the silence that followed she shifted uneasily in her chair.

"We wish to ask you," Rennert changed the subject, "about last night."

He felt the woman's eyes, like two black buttons set in her old skin, directed against his face. Her fingers were suddenly still.

"Did any of your guests visit you in your quarters?"

Her eyes were sharply speculative now.

"But yes, señor," she said after a momentary hesitation, "Miss Noon came."

"Why did she come?"

Madame Fournier's face became orderly and expressionless. Only her dark eyes probed Rennert's face.

"She came for a reading."

"I had forgotten your gifts along that line, madame."

Madame Fournier's tight lips relaxed a little.

"You will remember, Señor Rennert, that I once gazed into the crystal for you—when you were here before."

Rennert smiled.

"Yes, and your prediction came true. I returned to Taxco and to your house. It almost made a believer out of me."

"The Señor is gracious."

Captain Pérez interrupted impatiently:

"And this Miss Noon, madame—when did she go to your rooms?"

"It was after nine, señor, perhaps fifteen minutes after."

"And she stayed?"

"Only a few minutes. I was so disturbed by these things that have happened in the house that I could not concentrate upon the crystal."

She glanced inquiringly from one of them to the other.

"There is anything else the Señores wish to know? I have much to do downstairs."

"Do you know what time Riddle went to his room this morning?" Rennert asked as she made a movement to rise.

"No, señor. He ate breakfast about eight. I did not see him again until—" she broke off and fingered the fringes of the rebozo—"until I found him dead." Her fingers left the rebozo and made the sign of the cross.

"Do you know where he might have obtained the veronal?"

"Veronal?" She looked at him with an unreadable stare.

"Yes, there was veronal in the tablets which were on Riddle's table. Veronal is a drug, too much of which causes death."

"But no, señor, I do not know."

"Have you ever suspected, madame, that any of your guests were users of any kind of drugs?"

She spread her hands outward with a quick automatic gesture.

"But, Señor Rennert, I attend to my own business. The private affairs of my guests are none of my concern. You should know that."

"Certainly, but I thought that you might have—noticed some things."

She shook her head silently.

"You never suspected this Shaul of selling drugs?" Pérez asked.

"Shaul?" Her eyes left Rennert's face and fixed themselves on the calla lilies. "You think that he was selling the drugs?"

"A suspicion, nothing more," Rennert said.

The calculative look came again into her eyes.

"I do not know, señor." She spoke slowly and with a peculiar low emphasis to her words. "This Shaul had always much money."

"Did he seem to associate with any of the other guests in particular?"

She considered this a long time.

"He used to play cards with El Señor Crenshaw much," she said at last. "A game of you americanos—el poker."

"And how long has Crenshaw been in your house?" Rennert was trying to recall the date of Crenshaw's signature in the ledger downstairs.

"He came three days after Miss Noon, señor."

Rennert was immediately alert.

"And how do you remember this?"

"Because when he came he asked if this was the house where she was staying."

Rennert leaned back in his chair, his thoughts busy. Crenshaw had interested him from the first. The odd familiarity about his manner, his quick acquaintanceship with Riddle, his concern about the pillowcases found in the young man's room. He was not, distinctly, the type of American to whom a stay in Taxco would appeal . . . .

"There is nothing more, señores?" the woman asked again, getting to her feet and drawing the rebozo tight about her shoulders.

"I understand," Rennert said, "that an attempt was made to poison Mura this morning."

Madame Fournier leaned against the dresser, her fingers grasping at its edges as if for support. Stark, undisguised fear was in her eyes as she stared at his face.

"Yes, señor." She spoke with an effort.

"Who do you think did it?"

One hand left the dresser and stabbed wildly toward the floor.

"It was that cook, the ignorant one." The words came quickly, incoherently. "She put the poison in the tortillas and laid them down for Mura to eat. I heard her tell María last night that she was going to do it if Mura did not stop crying."

"And why do you think she wished Mura out of the way?"

Madame Fournier seemed absorbed in contemplation of the calla lilies. She was breathing quickly.

"It was because of something that Esteban told her," she said. "She is afraid of Mura—why, I do not know. And," she went on hastily, "I do not know why Esteban no longer likes Mura. He used to pet her, and she would follow him about. But now he has fear of her."

Rennert regarded her thoughtfully.

"And when did his attitude toward her change?"

"When he fell sick, señor, and heard her crying in the night."

"And he used the word 'nagual' on this occasion?"

"Yes, and again later." She made a choking noise in her throat and started toward the door.

"That will be all, madame," Rennert said, rising.

She fumbled with the knob, opened the door, and disappeared onto the balcony.

Rennert sat down and glanced at Pérez.

"The story of this Miss Noon is true, then." The Mexican spoke softly. "She was in the room of Madame Fournier when the young man visited hers."

"Yes," Rennert said, "I had a feeling that that was true, or she wouldn't have told something that could be checked up on so easily." He thrust a hand into his pocket for cigarettes. "This Crenshaw interests me now."

"Crenshaw?"

"Yes, I'd like very much to have a talk with him."

"Very well, señor." Pérez got up again and went to the door. While he was away Rennert wrote upon another sheet of paper the same word "nagual" and laid it upon the table. The Mexican returned and sat down. For several moments neither of them spoke.

"This poison in the food of the cat," Pérez asked at last, "what does it mean?"

Rennert had been thinking about this very matter. It worried him—like Madame's undisguised fear. He said: "I don't know, but I wish it had not been done."

He had probably let more seriousness creep into his voice than he realized, for he saw the Mexican regarding him intently.

"Can it be, Señor Rennert"—Rennert sensed the mockery in his tone—"that you think this cat is important?"

Rennert did not reply at once. Upon the tiles outside he heard the tread of approaching feet. He said: "I am beginning to believe, *mi capitán*, that this cat is very important in what is happening in this house."

Pérez laughed slightly.

"You have heard, I suppose, the old superstition that the cries of certain animals foretell death, that they can sense it in the air."

"Yes," Rennert carefully lowered his voice, "and I am about to believe that in this case at least the cat's screams actually *do* presage death."

The Mexican's eyes were fixed on his face when knuckles rapped sharply upon the door.

"You jest, Señor Rennert," he said, and called: "*Pase.*"

The door was thrown open, and Crenshaw entered.

Crenshaw was smoking a cigar. He held it gripped between his teeth in such a way that it emphasized his square protruding jaw. He stood for a moment in the doorway as his cold blue eyes went from Rennert to the officer. His face retained its composure, but there sprang into his eyes a faint look of surprise. He nodded and stepped forward.

"Well," he said as he sat down, "what's the idea of the meeting?"

"This"—Rennert indicated his companion with a nod—"is Captain Pérez. He is investigating the death of Mr. Riddle and has asked me to serve as interpreter for him."

Over the slow spirals of blue smoke that rose from the cigar Crenshaw's eyes were fixed appraisingly upon Rennert.

"I am to understand, then, that this is an official investigation?" A slight steel-like quality edged his voice.

"Yes, I have Captain Pérez's instructions for interrogation."

Crenshaw took the cigar from his mouth and stared thoughtfully at its gray cone of ash.

"What is it you want from me?"

"We had hoped," Rennert said, "that you might give us some information about Riddle's actions today."

With a careful movement Crenshaw flicked the ash onto the floor.

"Sure," he said, thrusting the cigar into his mouth again, "glad to tell you anything I can."

"Very well," Rennert said, "when did Riddle leave you this morning?"

"About ten forty-five, I should say. He came into my room after he left yours and stayed about half an hour. He told me that he was going to his own room then and try to get some sleep."

"Did you see him again?"

"No," Crenshaw's hesitation was barely discernible, "not alive."

"Your room is next to his, isn't it?"

Crenshaw nodded, and Rennert had the feeling that he was a fencer, rapier held steadily on guard.

"Do you know," he pursued, "if Riddle had any visitors after he left your room?"

"I couldn't say," Crenshaw's eyes seemed colder and bluer than ever, "but I know that he had an engagement for lunch at twelve-thirty."

"With whom?"

Crenshaw's eyes narrowed a trifle, went quickly to Captain Pérez, then back to Rennert.

"I don't know the drift of these questions," he said, "but I won't dispute your right to ask them, particularly since that guy has got a gun. His engagement was with Parkyn." He raised a hand peremptorily. "Wait a minute, now! I'll tell you all I know about it in a few words. When Riddle and I left this room this morning we went to mine, as I told you. Downstairs in the parlor we met Parkyn. He came up to Riddle and asked him if he could talk to him some time. Riddle didn't know who he was, and Parkyn had to remind him that he had met him out on the terrace last night, that you had introduced them, in fact. Riddle didn't seem very anxious to talk to Parkyn, but Parkyn insisted, and Riddle finally promised to eat lunch with him. Parkyn was going to stop by his room at twelve-thirty. And that," his manner as well as his words said, "is every damned thing I know about it."

Rennert asked: "Did Riddle ask Parkyn for some aspirin?"

Crenshaw's teeth sank slowly into his cigar. A bit of ash on the tip broke and fell upon his vest. He brushed it off without glancing down.

"Yes," he said, "he did. Parkyn said that he didn't have any."

The room was very, very quiet, and in the stillness Captain Pérez's chair creaked startlingly as he shifted his position. (*I wonder*, Rennert asked himself, *if the captain is bored or curious or indifferent to what is going on between this man and myself?*) Aloud he said: "What was the subject of your conversation with Riddle, Mr. Crenshaw?"

Crenshaw adjusted the cigar between his teeth again and drew upon it as he stared past Rennert's head.

"I think it's time," he said, "to tell you who I am and why I'm here in Taxco."

# CHAPTER TWELVE

## UNTIL TOMORROW

I WAS HOPING," Rennert said, "that you would decide to tell us exactly that."

Crenshaw's eyes came back to Rennert's face.

"Got me down as a suspicious character, haven't you?" He laughed slightly.

"Scarcely that, but I *have* been wondering what your real mission here was."

Crenshaw brought from an inner pocket a heavy manila envelope and handed it to Rennert.

"Here's my credentials. I brought them along in case they'd be needed."

Rennert opened the envelope and ran his eyes over the documents within. They certified that the bearer, whose photograph corresponded with that on the passport which accompanied them, was connected with a firm of private agents in Dallas, Texas. The firm was, Rennert was aware, one of the oldest and best known in the Southwest. He knew now why at his first meeting with Crenshaw there had been something vaguely familiar about the man. It was the unobtrusiveness of appearance, overlaying like a veneer a steely arrogance, which characterizes so many men of Rennert's own calling.

"I am acquainted with the reputation of your firm." He handed back the envelope.

Crenshaw nodded in matter-of-fact acknowledgment.

"I came down here," he said, "to conduct an investigation for Owen Riddle, the father of the young fellow who died this afternoon. As you may know, Riddle is a prominent oil man of Oklahoma, one of the richest, in fact. The Riddle field is named after him. The death of his son has, of course, put an end to my duties. I'm waiting now for instructions as to what he wants me to do."

The smoke from the cigar was a thin column distended by warm air that eddied in from the window.

"And the nature of this investigation?" Rennert asked.

Crenshaw's teeth tightened upon the cigar.

"Are you sure," he asked coldly, "that it has any bearing upon the boy's death?"

"It's possible," Rennert said evenly, "that it has. In view of that possibility, you would do well to tell us."

Crenshaw's eyes probed into his.

"Very well, it doesn't make any difference now, I suppose," he shrugged and the lines of his face relaxed a trifle. "The fact is that I came down here to get a line on this Gwendolyn Noon, who's staying in this house. The kid had fallen for her, and Riddle sent me to find out what kind of a woman she was. He's pretty strait-laced himself and didn't fancy the idea of his son bringing an actress into the family. He had an idea, too, that she might be making a play for some of the boy's money."

Rennert leaned forward in his chair.

"And just what have you learned about her?"

Crenshaw drew the cigar from his mouth and with his tongue flicked a particle of tobacco upon the floor.

"Just as the old man thought," he said, "she was after his money—there's no doubt about that. She had been married before and came down here to Mexico to get a divorce on the Q. T. so that Riddle wouldn't learn about husband number one."

"Have you reported this fact to him?"

"Not yet. I didn't get onto it until the other day."

"How did you happen to learn it?"

"From something Shaul said. It gave me the idea, and I had the office back home check up on it. As a matter of fact, I only heard from them yesterday."

"You knew Shaul well?"

Crenshaw hesitated.

"No, I can't say that I did. I used to play poker with him

once in a while, but except for that I didn't see much of him."

Rennert had the feeling that the other's tone was guarded. He asked: "What kind of man was he?"

Crenshaw stared for a moment at the end of the cigar, then thrust it between his teeth again.

"Rotten," he said succinctly.

"Do you want to amplify that?" Rennert asked.

Crenshaw shrugged.

"Everybody's got his own point of view, and far be it from me to criticize a man's morals, but Shaul was one I wouldn't trust farther than I could see. Personally, I think that who-ever killed him did the world a service."

Rennert leaned back in his chair and regarded Crenshaw thoughtfully.

"Did Stephen Riddle know about Gwendolyn Noon's pre-vious marriage?"

Crenshaw's pause was momentary.

"I told him this morning," he said.

"What was his reaction?"

Crenshaw smiled slightly.

"He got sore at me at first and told me to mind my own business; said that it made no difference to him if Noon had been married a dozen times, he loved her just the same and was going to marry her in spite of hell, high water, and his father. I tried to reason with him, but didn't have much luck. I thought I'd talk to him later, when he got some sleep and was calmed down."

"And Riddle never woke up," Rennert said slowly.

"No," Crenshaw said, "he never woke up. Must have taken too large a dose of the veronal."' He looked steadily at Ren-nert. "I examined the contents of those tablets," he said evenly, "that's why I know it was veronal."

"Have you any idea," Rennert asked, "where he may have gotten it?"

Crenshaw's eyes went slowly to the window, and the mus-cles about them tightened.

"I've got an idea, yes."

There was a moment of silence.

"Well?" Rennert prompted.

Crenshaw's voice was deliberate as he said: "Gwendolyn Noon is a dope head."

"I suspected that," Rennert said. "You think he may have gotten the veronal from her, then?"

Crenshaw shrugged.

"It's a natural supposition, isn't it?"

"Yes," Rennert said, "I suppose it is. But another supposition might be that Riddle had veronal of his own."

"No, I'm sure he hadn't," Crenshaw interposed quickly. "He asked me if I had any aspirin, said he had a headache and a hangover, and wanted to take some so he could go to sleep. I'm sure that if he had had any veronal he wouldn't have been asking for aspirin."

"You didn't give him any, then?"

"No, I didn't have any." His eyes left the window and fixed themselves on Rennert's. "He must have gone to someone else —Gwendolyn Noon, probably—after he left me and gotten the veronal from her. He was nervous and wrought up and could very easily have taken an overdose of it."

"You are sure, then, that he took the overdose by accident?"

Crenshaw slowly threw one long leg over the other and stared steadily at Rennert.

"You are insinuating, I suppose, that he committed suicide?"

"I was considering it as a possibility."

Crenshaw rolled the cigar about in his mouth.

"I don't think," he said at last, "that Riddle would have done that, though I may be wrong. I didn't meet him until last night, but he didn't strike me as the suicide type. Might talk about it, but that's all."

"Miss Noon broke her engagement with him yesterday."

"Yes," Crenshaw's frown was speculative, "he told me about that. He seemed to be sure he could win her back, though."

"Have you any idea why she broke the engagement?"

"Not the slightest." Crenshaw looked into his eyes quite frankly. "I'll admit it surprised me." He smoked for a moment in silence. "What difference does it make, anyway," he asked, "'which it was—accident or suicide? He's dead, and there's no use stirring up any more scandal. I'm sure old man Riddle would rather let the whole thing drop now—" he paused and seemed to be weighing his words before uttering them—"unless that pillowcase you found in his room means something."

Rennert said very carefully: "Shaul was smothered with that pillowcase last night while he was unconscious."

He watched Crenshaw's face. Not a muscle moved, and he sensed rather than saw the sudden tautening of the whole compact body.

"You have proof of that?" For the first time there was a trace of animation in Crenshaw's voice.

"That pillowcase," Rennert answered quietly, "constituted the proof. It disappeared from Shaul's room during the night."

"And it was found in Riddle's room this afternoon," Crenshaw spoke with slow deliberateness. For a moment he seemed lost in contemplation of his cigar. Then his voice quickened, "That's the idea, is it? That Riddle went to Shaul's room during the night and finished the job of killing him?"

"The theory had occurred to us, naturally. We wanted to know what you thought of it."

"As I told you, I only met Riddle last night. He was rather drunk then, so I can't tell you much about him. I should say, though, that it's even less likely that he would do that than that he would commit suicide. He was just an overgrown kid, after all."

"Very true. I'm inclined to think myself that Riddle was not the type to commit that murder. Still, it leaves the pillowcase unexplained."

"Maybe he heard that Shaul had been killed and was afraid he'd be accused of it, so he went and got the pillowcase during the night. It would be a perfectly natural action."

Rennert nodded thoughtfully. He was remembering that slight sound upon the balcony outside the half-open door of Shaul's room while he and Mrs. Giddings were within. That might have been Riddle.

"That is a possible explanation," he admitted.

They sat in silence for a moment. At length Crenshaw uncrossed his legs.

"Want me for anything else?"

"Just one more thing, Mr. Crenshaw. I've written a word

on that piece of paper over on the table. I wish that you would look at it and see if you recognize it."

Crenshaw got to his feet and walked over to the table. He stood, his hands thrust in his pockets, and looked down at the sheet of paper. He was frowning. He turned to Rennert and shook his head.

"Never saw it before, but that doesn't mean anything. I don't know a damn thing about Spanish."

"Very well, then, Mr. Crenshaw. That will be all."

Crenshaw's eyes met Rennert's in a steady level gaze.

"I know," he said, "that you haven't told me all about this affair, but far be it from me to butt in. In case you want my help, you've just got to let me know."

"Thanks," Rennert said, "we shall remember that."

Crenshaw turned and was gone. As the echoes of his thick-soled shoes died away upon the tiles, Captain Pérez looked inquiringly at Rennert.

Rennert summarized briefly the conversation. When he had concluded the Mexican looked at him and smiled. It was a pleasant smile, giving the impression at once of spontaneity, of studied effectiveness, of artificiality as only a Mexican smile can.

"There are other guests left to whom you have not talked?" The smile tempered yet did not hide the gentle raillery in the tone.

Rennert checked a sudden impulse and said: "Yes, there is; for example, Dr. Parkyn."

"Who had the appointment with the young man at twelve-thirty—the appointment which he did not keep."

"I was wondering," Rennert said evenly, "if perhaps he did keep the appointment."

"You wish him to be called then?" Pérez rose to his feet. The smile seemed fixed upon his face, and his teeth looked very white in the afternoon light.

"Yes," Rennert said.

This time the Captain did not reenter the room until he returned escorting Dr. Parkyn. When the archæologist came in, the same sheet of paper, bearing the same word, rested upon the top of the table.

The light struck the lenses of Parkyn's glasses and gave his face a curious mask-like appearance. He paused upon the threshold, glanced inquiringly at Rennert, said, "Good-afternoon," in a gruff voice, and sat down. His eyes now were seen as sharp and piercing, fixed on Rennert's face.

"I understand," he said, nodding toward Pérez, who had taken his seat, "that you and this general, or whatever he is, want to talk to me."

"Yes," Rennert said, "he is conducting the investigation into the death of Mr. Riddle and has asked me to serve as interpreter for him. His knowledge of English is slight."

"Well," Parkyn demanded abruptly, "what is it?"

"Riddle died, as you have doubtless heard, from an overdose of veronal. Captain Pérez has been trying to find out just when Riddle took the veronal. He understands that you had an appointment with him at twelve-thirty and wants to know if you kept it."

Parkyn's thick eyebrows were drawn together in a frown.

"Crenshaw told him, then?"

Rennert nodded.

"Well," Parkyn shrugged, "I'm afraid I can't help you any. I went to Riddle's room, as I told him I would, at twelve-thirty. I knocked at the door, but there was no answer. I knocked several times, then left. I thought that he had forgotten about the appointment. I looked for him downstairs but didn't see him any place."

"You did not enter his room?"

"No, of course not." Parkyn drew his pipe from the side pocket of his coat, took out a tobacco pouch and filled the bowl. Flakes of the tobacco showered to the floor.

"It has also been reported that Riddle asked you if you had any aspirin," Rennert continued, "and that you said you did not have."

"True." Parkyn squinted his eyes before the lighted match. "Crenshaw was with Riddle when he asked me."

"And you did not see Riddle again?"

"No." Parkyn flipped the match toward the window. It struck the sill and fell to the floor.

"I'm sure," Rennert said, "that you will not object to telling us the object of your appointment with Riddle."

Parkyn stared at the tiles where the match had fallen.

"I was going to take him to lunch with me," he said.

His pipe emitted short, quick puffs of blue smoke. His hands lay flat upon the arms of the chair, and he kept raising and lowering his fingers in a way that recalled, unpleasantly, the movements of a spider's legs.

"Did you know Riddle before he came here?" Rennert found his eyes following the movements of the fingers.

"No," Parkyn shook his head, "I never saw him before last night. You introduced us, remember?"

"Yes."

"Well, then," as Parkyn lowered his voice its gutturalness increased until it was barely intelligible, "any reason why I shouldn't pursue the acquaintance?"

"None at all," Rennert said pleasantly. "This is just routine work with Captain Pérez, you understand."

"Of course, of course," Parkyn got to his feet. "That will be all, then?"

"Just one more thing, Dr. Parkyn. Over on that table is a sheet of paper upon which I have written the word which Esteban is said to have been using. I should appreciate it if you would glance at it and tell me if I have spelled it correctly."

Parkyn shot him a sharp inquiring glance, then went to the table and picked up the paper. He put it down almost at once and turned to Rennert.

"That's right, though it's sometimes spelled n-a-u-a-l. The 'g' is not pronounced, ordinarily."

"Thank you," Rennert said, "sorry to be have bothered you."

"No bother at all," Parkyn said as he went past him. "Have I helped you in establishing the time of the boy's death?"

"Yes," Rennert said, "I think you have."

"He was—dead when I was knocking at his door?"

"Yes, he was dead when you were knocking at his door."

Parkyn was staring at the floor. "Too bad," he said, "that I didn't know it, but I don't suppose I could have helped him any then." He turned and walked to the door. Rennert never knew whether the slam was accidental or intentional.

He said: "This man's story is that he had an appointment with Riddle at twelve-thirty. He was going to take him to lunch. He went to his room at that time and knocked at the door. There was no answer, so he left."

Captain Pérez smiled again.

"And now, Señor Rennert," he spoke pleasantly, "I have kept my promise. I have permitted you to question these people. And the result?" He spread his hands dramatically. "Nothing! You have no proof that this young man did not commit suicide. As to whether he murdered the other man or not—that is not important now."

"But we have not found out where he got the veronal."

Pérez shrugged. "Perhaps he had some all the time and took it when he could not obtain aspirin. Perhaps one of these people gave it to him but does not wish to admit it now. Are you satisfied?"

Rennert looked into the mountains and smiled.

"No," he said with a note of seriousness that belied the smile, "I am not. I believe that in this house there is a person who accomplished—by some means or other—the deaths of both Shaul and Riddle. If we drop the case now, that person will go free as soon as the quarantine is lifted."

Captain Pérez's fingers slowly turned the ring upon his left hand. His face retained its impassivity, but in his dark eyes there was a worried look. *He is wishing,* Rennert thought, *that I had never come to Taxco, or at least not to the house of Madame Fournier. Then the whole matter could be comfortably dropped.*

"Señor Rennert," Pérez said at last, his voice more liquid than ever, "I want to see that justice is done to your countrymen, as I have told you. But I am satisfied that there is nothing more to be learned about this case. Still, if you wish to continue the investigation here, you have my permission." His eyes rose to meet Rennert's. "Is that satisfactory?"

Rennert nodded slowly.

"*Bueno,*" he said, "let us leave it so. In spite of myself I am beginning to become interested in the affair. It has angles that I didn't suspect at first. I may count on you for aid and coöperation in case I need it?"

"Assuredly, señor," the Mexican responded with alacrity.

"Very well. Do you have any fingerprint experts here in Taxco?"

"But what would you, Señor Rennert?" The Mexican's smile was deprecatory. "In this town we do not have the need."

"In Cuernavaca, I suppose, prints can be compared?"

"Yes, I believe so."

Rennert laid a newspaper flat upon the top of the table. He went to the center of the room and with his handkerchief carefully unscrewed the electric light bulb. He placed it on the newspaper, then went to his trunk. From one of the drawers he took the candle which he had carried from Shaul's room the night before and from which he had carefully removed the wax which had melted and run down the sides. He put this beside the bulb. From the volume of Tennyson he removed (after careful inspection) two sheets of notepaper. He added them and the sheet which Parkyn had held to the assortment upon the newspaper. He wrapped up the whole and handed the bundle to the Mexican.

"I have initialed each of these sheets of paper," he said. "If you will have them examined you will find, I believe, that one of them bears fingerprints that correspond to those on both the candle and the electric light bulb. The person who visited Shaul's room last night and smothered him left marks on the wax of the candle, unless I am greatly mistaken. The same person, unless again I am mistaken, unscrewed the light bulb in this room. How soon can you let me know the result?"

"By tomorrow, I believe, Señor Rennert." Pérez was holding the bundle rather uncertainly. His eyes were fixed upon it. "You asked each of these people to look at the word which you wrote in order to get their fingerprints?"

"Yes, and to watch their reactions to blotting paper."

"To blotting paper?" The Mexican glanced up inquiringly.

Rennert told him of the mutilated pad which he had found in Shaul's room.

"This Mr. Shaul wrote something in ink which someone did not wish to be seen, then. Is that your theory?"

Rennert laughed.

"Frankly, I have no theory as yet."

Pérez adjusted the bundle under his arm.

"That means"—he looked Rennert straight in the face—"that you suspect one of the people who was in this room within the last hour."

Rennert nodded and said grimly: "Yes, I suspected two of them. Now I am inclined to eliminate one."

"You noticed that Mr.—I do not remember his name—the first man who came in——"

"Crenshaw," Rennert supplied.

"Ah, yes, Crenshaw. You noticed that he did not pick up the sheet of paper?"

"Yes," Rennert said, "I didn't fail to notice that." He paused. "Have you any idea how long this quarantine is going to last?"

"The regular doctor returns from Mexico City tomorrow. He should be here at noon or before. We shall know then what it is that the sick boy has. If it is the smallpox," he shrugged, "the quarantine will probably last for a long time."

"You will have the doctor come here as soon as he arrives in Taxco?"

"Yes, at once." Pérez arose and faced Rennert. "Until noon tomorrow, then, señor. And in the meantime guard yourself well against this murderer of yours." He extended a hand.

Rennert grasped it, smiling, and walked to the door with the Mexican.

"*Hasta mañana, capitán.* And when you bring the doctor you might bring also a pair of handcuffs."

As they stood there upon the threshold the silence that lay about the house and the hillside was split by the screaming of the Siamese cat. It was loud—frenzied and unnatural in its intensity.

The Mexican's eyes searched Rennert's face as the cries were suddenly cut off.

"You were serious, señor," the subdued tone lent sibilance to his speech, "in what you said about the screams of the cat?"

Rennert said: "At the time I didn't know whether I was serious or not—but now I am beginning to believe that I was."

The Mexican, he knew, was undecided as to whether or not he was being "kidded." He solved the question neatly with a shrug and walked down the balcony toward the stairs.

Rennert stood for a moment at the door, staring out into the hot bright sunlight that bathed the hillside and smiling grimly to himself at the strange fancy that had crept upon him—that the screaming of the Siamese cat had carried in it an undertone of mockery almost human.

# CHAPTER THIRTEEN

### THE CUP AND THE LIP

Mrs. GIDDINGS was standing upon the balcony outside her room, staring down the hillside. Her shoulders were stooped, and her hands hung listlessly at her sides, as if her thin frame lacked the energy to move them. Her face, seen in profile, looked tired and drawn.

She looked around as Captain Pérez passed her, caught sight of Rennert, and smiled wanly. He walked toward her.

"Good-evening, Mr. Rennert."

"Good-evening, Mrs. Giddings. I have not seen you today." He stood by the railing.

"No, I have been with Esteban most of the time. I just came out for a breath of fresh air—and to rest for a few minutes, looking at the cathedral. At this time of day I think it is most beautiful, with the sun's rays glinting against it."

"Yes." Rennert turned his head and followed her gaze to the twin towers of pink stone and the multi-colored dome of tiles that rose like some vivid tropical flower from the tops of the laurel trees in the plaza. "I always feel that it is going to fade away—like a mirage, before my eyes."

She was slowly intertwining her long, fragile-looking fingers.

"That's it—"she spoke softly—"a mirage. And like most of the beauty of life, one keeps expecting to see it fade away."

He studied her covertly. *This is not the same woman,* he was thinking, *who told me in such a matter-of-fact voice that Shaul was dead.*

"In Taxco, at least, it does not fade," he said.

"No," a trace of bitterness was in her voice, "but it is like life, too, in that its beauty is built upon ugly things. What made that church, this town, possible? The slavery of thousands of Indians who labored to build it and to bore into these mountains for silver. Just so that old José de la Borda might ease his conscience before God and that we might sit here and rest our eyes. Like life, it isn't worth so much pain and suffering." She looked up at Rennert and laughed in a low, throaty fashion. "Excuse me," she said, "for talking that way, but I've been feeling moody today—too tired, I suppose."

Rennert had seen the lines etched deeply about her eyes.

"Why don't you get some rest?" he asked. "Surely there is no need for you to stay with Esteban so closely."

She turned her face and stared again down the hillside.

"I know," she said in a low, almost inaudible tone, "but it gives me some purpose in my existence here, a daily round to go through with. I really welcome the opportunity to be doing something useful, and it tires me out so that I get occasional snatches of sound sleep. I slept almost three hours last night, without awakening—something I haven't done since I've been here."

Rennert waited. She did not continue. He asked: "How is Esteban this afternoon?"

She shook her head slowly.

"Still worse. He has given up hope and is waiting to die. He was delirious this afternoon. That was when Dr. Parkyn was wanting to see him. I wouldn't let him, of course. About an hour ago Esteban heard the cat screaming and was so frightened that I had to give him a sedative. He is sleeping now."

"Do you know why Dr. Parkyn wished to talk to Esteban?"

"No, he didn't say. He was insistent, though. Very insistent. He made me promise to let him know as soon as he could talk with him."

"What is your opinion," Rennert asked carefully, "about Esteban's illness? It seems strange that there should be so much uncertainty about it."

She brushed a hand across her forehead. Her eyes were momentarily closed.

"That's one thing which makes it so bad—this uncertainty. I was sure that is was the measles or smallpox, but the rash doesn't seem to be spreading. Now I don't know what to think about it, and I don't think this doctor does either." She hesitated. "I am almost ready to believe the cook—that this house has a curse upon it. It's probably my imagination, but I have the feeling that there is death here. Death, like some of these Mexican toys you see on All Souls' Day, impish. It's as if he were indulging in some terrible game just for his own sport, keeping us here and sorting us out for his victims. Just at his own whim."

Rennert glanced at her sharply. There had been a suppressed note of hysteria in her voice.

"See here," he said, "you've got to be careful—you're letting your imagination run away with you."

"No," her thin lips parted slightly, "it's not my imagination altogether. It's the little disturbing things that keep happening in this house. Any one of them wouldn't be so bad, but, taken all together, they make me afraid."

Rennert felt a sudden alertness of the senses.

"Suppose you tell me," he suggested, "just what little disturbing things you mean."

With one hand she gestured vaguely in the direction of the terrace.

"You will think it silly of me, I suppose, and I hope you're right." She hesitated. "In the first place," her voice quickened as if with forced resolve, "it was the attempt to poison the cat." She looked up at him with eyes filmed by tears. "You heard about that?"

"Yes, I understand that some kind of poison was put into her food."

"It was arsenic." Her voice sank. "Madame Fournier kept a supply of it in the kitchen, to kill rats. It always rested on a shelf above the stove. I was in the kitchen preparing some broth for Esteban this morning and noticed that the box was gone. I told Madame and, I suppose, caught some of her fear. She was terribly agitated. A few minutes later she found that someone had left a plate of tortillas in her room for the cat. She brought them out. They had been sprinkled with arsenic."

Her hands were twisting and untwisting now. "I am wondering"—Rennert had to lean forward in order to hear the words
—"if all the arsenic was put in those tortillas or whether there
is more about the house somewhere."

"What is your idea about who tried to poison the cat?"

She stared fixedly at the tiles.

"I suppose," she said, "that Madame Fournier is right—
that it was Micaela, the cook. She has always been afraid of
Mura, for some reason. She denied having done it, but Madame
found proof that she had been in her room this morning."

"What was this proof?" Rennert asked quickly.

"You know that Madame keeps a collection of Indian idols
and masks and curios to sell to tourists who come to Taxco.
The most valuable ones are in her room. One of the masks—
a little jade one—was missing this morning. Later she found it
hidden out in the kitchen. She thinks that is proof that the
cook was in her room."

"But why this morning?"

"Because she says she is sure the mask was in its place last
night."

"Has this cook been here long?" Rennert asked after an
instant.

"No, I think not."

Rennert was silent for a moment.

"Was there anything else?" he asked.

"Yes," she kept her eyes averted, "there was the doctor's
instrument case."

Rennert stared at her.

"Tell me about that."

"Well," she shrugged with a little gesture of helplessness, "it
may not mean anything, but it disappeared this afternoon. He
left it in the sala when he went in to see Esteban. When he
came back, it was gone. I found it a few minutes ago, in the
sala, where he said that he had left it."

Rennert's voice was steady.

"What did you do with it?"

"I have it in my room. I'll give it to the doctor when he
returns."

"You don't know, then, whether or not there was anything missing from it?"

"No." Her lips formed the monosyllable very slowly.

Rennert regarded her thoughtfully.

"Has there been anything else?"

She was staring unseeingly in the direction of the cathedral.

"The other thing," she said, "is, I suppose, too insignificant to mention. But coming together with these other things—"

"Suppose you tell me."

"It was Madame Fournier's crystal," she said.

"Her crystal?"

"Yes, the crystal ball that she gazes into during her séances. It was broken last night."

"She told you?"

"No, I went into her room this morning, when she found the poisoned tortillas. It was lying under the table in a corner of the room—broken to pieces."

"Did she offer any explanation?"

"No, I don't think that she knew I saw it."

"A worse omen"—Rennert's smile was grim—"than a broken mirror, I suppose, if one is superstitiously inclined."

"Yes," Mrs. Giddings said. She loosened her hands with a motion that was almost a jerk. "And you will think that I am as superstitious as the old Mexican cook if I keep on like this. I must go back to Esteban." She laid a hand on Rennert's shoulder. "Forgive me," she said, "but I had to have someone to talk to. It was today—coming after last night. This Mr. Riddle—was that murder, too?"

Rennert's eyes met hers.

"Yes, Mrs. Giddings," he said gravely, "I am convinced that it was murder."

She ran her tongue over dry, tight lips.

"I had a feeling that it was," she said. Her eyes searched his. "Do you know yet who—who is doing this?"

"No, I had been hoping that you might be of assistance."

"I?" She stood suddenly very still. "How could I be of assistance?"

"By gossiping a bit about your fellow guests here. You know

them better than I do, and should"—he watched her face—
"have certain suspicions."

She moved a step forward, like an automaton, and rested
both hands upon the railing.

"Last night," she said, "I went over everybody in this house
and tried to picture each one of them as a murderer. I couldn't
do it, not as planning a cold-blooded murder, but this would
have been so easy—while Shaul lay there unconscious. He—or
she—may just have acted on an impulse."

"She?"

"Yes," she nodded slowly, "there's no use mincing matters.
A woman could have done it as well as a man."

"Which brings us—still without mincing matters—to whom?"

She glanced backward at the door beyond the stairs.

"You think," Rennert interpreted, "that Miss Noon may have
done it?"

"I would as soon have suspected her as anyone else before
this young man's death today." Her voice was cold and deliberate. "After all, why this eternal instinct to shield women—
particularly beautiful women—from unpleasant things? A
woman can hate more thoroughly, more intensely than ever a
man can. And when a woman's inhibitions are loosened, as
Miss Noon's are——" she did not finish.

"You have noticed her condition, then?" Rennert asked.

"Yes, of course."

"When did you first suspect that she was a user of drugs?"

"About the time she was deprived of her supply, about two
weeks ago."

"She hasn't had any since then?"

"I think that she has gotten it from time to time, but irreg-
ularly. The last few days I think that she has had none at all.
I feel sorry for her at times."

"Do you have any idea where she used to get the drugs?"

"No, none at all."

"Nor why she ceased to be able to get them?"

"No, unless it was on account of lack of money."

"She was hard up, then?"

"She asked me once to loan her some money. That was about

a week ago. I couldn't, not for that purpose. I suspected, you see, what she would do with it."

Silence stood between them for a moment.

"What was your impression of Donald Shaul?" Rennert asked.

She did not reply for a moment.

"A particularly despicable man," she said with a slight shrug, "although, if you pressed me for a reason for saying that, I'd have to admit that it is just a woman's intuition. I didn't know him more than casually."

"And how did Miss Noon act toward him?"

"I think that she was afraid of him—and I think that she hated him. I saw her looking at him once down in the dining room. It was only a glance, but I don't think I ever saw such concentrated hate in one person's eyes."

"You know of no one else who had particular cause to hate him?"

"No, I don't think that anyone liked him, but as far as I know, no one's feelings went beyond dislike."

She glanced down toward the door of the sala.

"But I must go and see if Esteban is resting. You will let me know as soon as you can, won't you? It will relieve this strain of living under the same roof with a person who has committed a murder—without knowing which person it is."

"Yes," Rennert said, "I shall let you know as soon as possible. In the meantime, I think it might be better if you gave me that instrument case. I shall deliver it to the doctor when he comes."

"All right." She went into her room and returned in a moment, carrying in her hand a small black case. She handed it to Rennert. "Do you think," she asked, "that it is—a part of all the rest of this?"

Rennert said very carefully. "I think that it is a very integral part."

She said in an odd voice: "I'm glad that I am being of some help," turned quickly, and walked toward the stairs.

*It is a specter,* Rennert thought as he watched her, *that prevents her from sleeping, but it is an intangible one. Therefore she has identified it with these very real, not at all imaginary*

*ripples made by whatever rapacious undercurrents are sweeping
about this house.*

As he walked to his room he was trying to catalogue in their
places the cat's poisoned food, the briefly missing instrument
case, and the shattered crystal. He locked the case in a drawer
of his trunk, then crossed to the left wing. He entered Riddle's
room and closed the door behind him.

The bed had not been made since the removal of the body,
and there was something vaguely disquieting about the way
the pillow still bore the impress of Riddle's head. He might
just have lifted it after sound, healthy sleep.

Upon the dresser stood another Puebla bowl filled with the
same yellow flowers that he had seen in Shaul's room. The air
was close and mephitic with their odor. Rennert went to the
window and threw it open.

Riddle had not yet unpacked his belongings, and his suitcase
stood open upon the floor. Rennert examined its contents with
practised fingers. It contained nothing but the barest necessities
of traveling, evidently hastily thrown together.

He made sure that the closet and the dresser were empty,
then went to the little bedside table. He pulled open the single
drawer and took from it an envelope which lay upon a stack of
notepaper. The letter was addressed in slightly blurred handwriting to Mr. Owen Riddle, at Tulsa, Okla., and bore no
stamp. It was unsealed. Rennert held it in his hands for several
moments, considering, before taking out the contents. These
consisted of a single sheet of paper upon which were scrawled
these words:

Taxco, June 17.

DEAR DAD:

I just talked to the man you sent down here to spy on
Gwendolyn. If he has not told you yet he soon will, so I
might as well say what I've got to say right now. He says
that she is married and that she is here in Taxco waiting
for a divorce so that she can marry me. I haven't asked her
yet if it's true or not because it doesn't make any difference
to me. I am going to marry her anyway, or if she can't get
the divorce and will have me anyway I'll be satisfied. I
know what your ideas are about those things, so there's no

use going over that again. A fraternity brother of mine in Mexico City has promised me a job with a construction company any time I want it. I'm going to take it. So you don't need to worry about having to spend any more money on me. I haven't any hard feelings toward you, and, I suppose, I'll write you again sometime. You just don't know Gwendolyn.

Yours,<br>STEPHEN.

Rennert stared thoughtfully at the letter, folded it, and slipped it into the envelope. After a moment's thought he put it into his pocket.

"Oh, hello there!"

Rennert looked up quickly as a deep voice spoke from the doorway in the west wall.

Mandarich's bulk seemed to fill the door as he stood with his hands jammed in his pockets. He wore neither coat nor vest, and his shirt sleeves were rolled up to expose thick, powerfully muscled forearms, covered with short, wiry hairs.

"Good-evening," Rennert said, "did I disturb you?"

"Heard somebody moving around in this room and thought I'd see who it was." Mandarich's eyes were candid and blue behind the tortoise-shell glasses, but Rennert had the feeling that they had rested for a fraction of a second upon his coat pocket. "Thought it might be one of these damn thieving Mexicans trying to get away with something."

Rennert smiled.

"I have the permission of the captain of police in charge here."

"Of course." The artist's large round face was creased by a pleasant smile. "I wouldn't have opened the door if I had known it was you in here."

Rennert's eyes went past him and to the room beyond the bathroom.

"I'm through here," he said. "Do you mind if I talk to you a few minutes?"

Mandarich thrust his hands deeper into his pockets, and

Rennert had the curious feeling that he was about to lunge forward, like a top-heavy statue.

"Of course not," Mandarich said, "come on in my room. It will be more pleasant there." He stood aside for Rennert to pass. "In fact, I'd be glad to know what in the hell is going on in this place."

Rennert passed through the diminutive bathroom and into the room beyond. He sat down.

"Have a drink?" Mandarich asked.

Rennert assented and surveyed the room as the other moved heavily across the floor to a large wardrobe of some dark wood, dulled by age, that stood against the west wall.

Mandarich set small glasses of blue Jalisco ware and two bottles upon the table at Rennert's elbow.

"What'll it be?" he asked. "Whisky or cognac?"

"Cognac," Rennert replied; "make it a light one."

Mandarich picked up the bottle of Three Star Hennessey and tilted it over one of the glasses.

"It's made me a little nervous," he said, his eyes upon the liquid, "that kid dying in the room right next to mine." He set the bottle upon the table and inserted the cork. "What was the trouble? An overdose of something, I heard."

"An overdose of veronal," Rennert said.

Mandarich was pouring himself a drink from the bottle of Scotch whisky. He took it in his hand and sank heavily into a chair that seemed too frail for his weight.

He held his glass up to the light and stared into its depths. Rennert thought that his eyes narrowed slightly.

"Veronal?" he repeated. "So that's what he found?"

Something in his voice made Rennert glance at him quickly.

"Why?" he asked. "Was he looking for some?"

Mandarich tilted back his head and drained the glass. He leaned forward and set it upon the table, moving his tongue over his lips as he did so.

"He came in here a few minutes after noon and asked me if I had any aspirin. I hadn't. He started to go out, then asked me if I had anything that would put him to sleep quick. He seemed kind of desperate, said that he had to have some sleep. I didn't have a thing."

"What did he do then?"

"He went back to his room. I heard him go out in a few minutes."

"And he came back?"

"In five or six minutes, I think."

Rennert watched Mandarich's face. He asked: "Did you hear any further sounds in his room?"

He thought that Mandarich was about to frown. However, his brow remained smooth as he said with a slight laugh: "I was busy writing and didn't pay any particular attention to what was going on in there. I did, though, hear someone knocking at his door a few minutes after he came back. Riddle called, 'Come in,' I know, and he and this other person exchanged a few words. I think the other fellow went out then."

"It was a man, then?" Rennert was alert.

"Yes."

"Do you know who it was?"

Again he had the feeling that Mandarich was about to give vent to anger or displeasure. But again there came that soft laugh.

"No," he said, "I don't know. I was writing and didn't pay any particular attention."

Rennert saw Mandarich's eyes on his still full glass. He was conscious that he had forgotten the drink which the artist had poured for him. He picked up the glass and held it to his lips. He felt an immediate alertness of the senses and was conscious that his eyes had gone quickly, suspiciously, to Mandarich's face. He set the glass back upon the table and adjusted his lips in a smile.

"Do you mind," he said, "if I change my mind and take whisky? I had forgotten it was so near dinner time. Whisky always goes better with me before a meal."

For a fraction of a second he saw a queer startled look in Mandarich's eyes as they stared at him.

"Of course," the man said, arising. "Sure there's nothing wrong with that cognac?"

Rennert laughed.

"With Hennessey cognac? Impossible!"

Mandarich walked across the room to the wardrobe, opened

one of the glass-paneled doors, and brought out another glass.

"See here," he said as he filled it from the bottle of whisky, "why all the questions? It strikes me that there's something damn mysterious going on in this house."

Rennert's face kept a careful lack of expression.

"Why?" he asked.

Mandarich poured himself another glass of whisky and sat down. He drained it at one long gulp. Rennert followed suit and returned the glass to the table.

"Well—" Mandarich hesitated and looked at him uncertainly —"I don't like to talk about one of your friends."

Something in his voice, an undertone of raillery, it might have been, puzzled Rennert.

"I'm afraid," he said, "that I don't understand." Suddenly he wondered whether Mandarich were drunk. Yet the man's hands seemed steady enough, and his tongue showed no indication of thickness.

"It's that Noon woman I mean," Mandarich said. Something about the way he drew his thick lower lip back against his teeth gave his full-moon face a lewd expression.

Rennert stared at him thoughtfully.

"I never met Miss Noon until yesterday," he said.

Mandarich rubbed the palms of his hands together with a slight rotary motion.

"Fast work, then, I'd say," he commented.

Rennert's voice hardened a bit.

"Still I don't understand what you mean."

"Let it go, let it go." Mandarich shrugged. "Have another drink."

"No, thanks."

Mandarich laughed.

"Don't get sore about it," he said. "It's my first experience with *une femme fatale.*"

"Meaning Miss Noon?"

"Yes."

"And why," Rennert asked, "do you think that such a melodramatic description fits her?"

Mandarich laughed again.

"She belongs," he said, gesturing with one hand, "in the

company of that queen of whom Francois Villon sang—the Queen of Burgundy whose beauty was a death trap—with the sirens of Acapulco, and so forth. She has at least made Taxco more interesting this spring."

"Do you mind," Rennert asked, "being more explicit?"

"About the Queen of Burgundy or Miss Noon?"

"About Miss Noon. I've read Villon."

"Well," Mandarich sank back comfortably in his chair, "she certainly seems to have had an attraction for the men about this house. There was Shaul—he's dead. There was Riddle—he's dead. There was Parkyn—he's still alive. And now you come along."

Rennert asked: "Parkyn was attracted to Miss Noon?"

Mandarich smiled knowingly.

"He fell for her, yes."

"And the result?"

"She didn't seem to appreciate the honor. In fact, it was rumored that the lady just laughed at him when he made the well-known advances. It rather wounded his vanity, I think. I judge he has always fancied himself rather a Don Juan among the ladies."

Rennert thought a moment.

"And why," he asked curiously, "do you include me among those smitten by the lady's charms?"

Mandarich got up and walked over to the table. He picked up the bottle of whisky and held it up suggestively.

"No more for me," Rennert said.

Mandarich poured himself another glassful.

"I happened to be out on the balcony last night," he said as he sat down again. "I saw you two come out of Shaul's room. It struck me as rather a gruesome place for a rendezvous, but there's no accounting for tastes, I suppose."

Rennert stared at him.

"You were smoking," he asked, "a cigarette?"

"Yes, I believe I was."

"And the time?"

"I'm not sure. It was after eleven, though, because the electric lights had been turned off. I saw you by the light of the candle in Shaul's room."

For an instant Rennert had the feeling that he should not have drunk the whisky. The whole affair had suddenly fallen out of focus, as if a lens had been jarred. Whom had he seen upon that balcony—Riddle or Mandarich? If it had been Mandarich, what had Riddle's words meant? He recalled the eagerness with which Riddle had told of his view of the pillowcase in the hand of the person who emerged from Shaul's room. He recalled his admission, perhaps not as reluctant as it had seemed, that Miss Noon had not been in her room when he had gone there. Was it possible that the young man had deliberately tried to direct suspicion against her? To what purpose? There was, Rennert told himself, only one answer—to shield himself. A weak-willed person such as Riddle had undoubtedly been, seeing himself endangered, might in panic or calculatedly have taken this means to insure his own safety. And then Riddle's death. . . .

He got up. (If it were the whisky a turn or two in the fresh air would clear his head.) His eyes rested momentarily upon the bottle of cognac and the still full glass as he said: "My meeting with Miss Noon was purely accidental, yet I don't yet have so many gray hairs that I would wish it otherwise."

Mandarich, too, rose from his chair. "Better have another drink before you go," he suggested, smiling.

Rennert said: "No, thank you," and left the room. He stood upon the balcony and breathed deeply of Taxco's warm air. For he knew that but a fraction of an inch had separated his lips from sudden, retching death.

## CHAPTER FOURTEEN

### THE SUN SETS IN STILLNESS

Rennert knocked at the door of Madame Fournier's apartment. He thought that he heard inside a soft movement, as if a piece of furniture had been moved upon the floor, but the handle of the door remained motionless. Again a sound from within, this time as of a heavy person walking on tiptoe, and as he stood and gazed at the intricate carvings in the ancient, worm-bored wood, he knew that Madame was standing on the other side and, like himself, listening. He even believed that he could hear labored breathing.

He knocked again.

"Who's there?" He scarcely recognized the low voice within as that of Madame Fournier.

He gave his name. There was a momentary pause, then a key grated in the lock, and the door was opened.

Madame Fournier stood in front of him, the fingers of one hand tightly clutched about the door knob. She wore a flame-colored dressing gown and, Rennert judged at a glance, no corset, for her body was without contours. Her hair, for once, was uncovered by the lace cap, and Rennert realized with something of a start that it was almost entirely gray. She looked, as she stared at him with sunken eyes, incredibly older than she had the brief space of twenty-four hours before.

"Ah, Señor Rennert! Come in." There was ill-disguised relief in her tone.

Rennert stepped into the room and watched her close and lock the door.

"You have fear, madame," he said to her in Spanish.

She moved across the room with slow uncertain steps and sank into a huge cushioned chair. She sat as if seeking respite in its depths and looked at him. Her eyes seemed the only part of her face that lived. They were alert and crafty as they searched his face.

"No, señor." She might have been a swimmer just risen to the surface and avid for breath. "Of what should I have fear?"

Rennert sat in a rush-bottomed chair with a wooden back that had been painted a pale blue. He gazed for an instant about the room. It was small and had a cluttered effect. The walls were painted the same color as the back of the chair and had at their junction with the ceiling a broad band of red. The chamber had no windows, and light from the adjoining room filtered through a bead-and-bamboo curtain before the open door. Against the opposite wall stood a huge wooden cabinet upon whose shelves were ranged pottery, stone idols, masks,

and other objects whose identity Rennert could not distinguish
in the dim light.

"Is it your habit, then, to keep your door locked during the
day?" he asked, conscious of her scrutiny.

She straightened herself in the chair and put one hand to her
hair. It shoved ineffectually at the straggling locks. Her laugh
was inadequate.

"I wanted to sleep, señor. Last night I could not. And I did
not wish to be disturbed. Micaela, the cook, and María, they
have always a thousand questions to ask, they cannot think for
themselves."

"They come, then, to your room?"

"But, yes, señor," she nodded, keeping her eyes on his face.

"I understand," Rennert said carefully, "that it was Micaela
who put out the poison for Mura."

Her eyes flashed.

"Yes." She murmured something unintelligible in French.
"As soon as this quarantine is over so that I can get a new cook,
Micaela goes."

"And why are you so positive that it was Micaela?"

"It was a mask, señor, a jade mask." She gestured toward
the cabinet. "She took it from there this morning. I found it
hidden in the kitchen. It is proof that she was in this room."

"But," Rennert insisted, "not that she tried to poison Mura."

"But," sudden energy seemed to flow into her body, "Micaela
has always had fear of Mura; she has not wanted to stay in the
same room with her. And she had no business in here."

"How does she account for the mask being in the kitchen?"

"She lies, like all these Mexicans. She shakes her head and
says: 'No sé, senora; no sé, señora!' " She went into elaborate
pantomime and spat out the phrases in rapid staccato.

"May I see the mask?" Rennert asked.

She stared at him for a moment, as if uncomprehending.

"But yes, if you wish. It is there," gesturing, "in the center
of the upper shelf."

Rennert walked to the cabinet and took from the place which
she had indicated a jade mask, perhaps six inches high. It rep-
resented a grotesque, full-lipped face, with narrow rounded cavi-
ties for eyes. The reverse was a squat deity with a fantas-

tic headdress who bore in his left hand a peculiar oblong implement.

"What is it, madame?" Rennert asked as he carried it toward the door.

"Just a little jade mask from the Indians of the mountains. There are others on that shelf. But you have seen them before, Señor Rennert. The tourists like to buy them."

Rennert was studying the mask.

"Is this different from your others?"

"The figure is different, yes, and the carving is better—but there are others larger."

"You don't happen to know what kind of an Aztec deity this is supposed to represent, do you?"

She shrugged.

"But no, señor, I know nothing of those things. For the tourists who come, yes, I tell them stories about them. But you are an old friend, Señor Rennert, and you I tell that I know nothing about these things."

"Where did you get this mask?"

"From some Indian who brought it in from the mountains. He said that he found it in a cave on the other side of the Huitzteco."

Rennert yielded to an impulse.

"Will you sell it to me, madame?"

A puzzled frown corrugated her forehead.

"But, Señor Rennert," protest was in her voice, "why do you want it? I have others—of jade, also—larger, more beautiful."

"I'd like to have this one," Rennert gazed down at it and smiled grimly, "as a souvenir of this spring, let us say."

Madame Fournier laughed without reserve.

"But, yes, then, señor, take it, if you wish. At least I do not sell you fakes like those storekeepers down on the plaza."

"How much?" Rennert slipped the mask into the pocket of his coat.

Madame Fournier seemed to be regaining her spirits. She smiled at him indulgently.

"If you were a tourist who came here I should say ten pesos, but you I charge only what I paid the Indian for it. A *tostón*."

Rennert took from his pocket a fifty-centavos coin and laid it upon the table.

"I always suspected," he said with a grin, "that there was a profit in these things. If the depression keeps up back in the States I'll come to Mexico and start a curio store."

She favored him with another smile, and the mole on her chin went up and down.

"There is profit, yes, señor."

She spoke abstractedly, staring at the doorway, where the Siamese cat had appeared. As Mura peered through the curtain at Rennert, her black triangular face might have been an odd pendant upon the bead-and-bamboo strings.

"Perhaps," Rennert said, "you would give me a séance and tell me what your crystal foretells for me in case I went into such a business."

Madame Fournier's face was tautened again by fear, and her eyes seemed to sink once more into their craters.

"The crystal," she whispered, "it is broken, señor."

"Broken?" Rennert showed surprise.

"Yes, it is broken. Mura broke it last night."

"And that is what you fear, madame?"

She stared at him and said, with low emphasis on the words: "Yes, señor, that is why I have fear. It is bad luck." She repeated it in a low, almost inaudible voice: *"Mala suerte!"*

The Siamese cat raised a black forepaw and beat the air as she screamed. The suddenness of it made Rennert start. Heard in the confines of the little room, it had a raucous quality about it that was almost unbearable in its intensity. It ended in a low growl.

"Poor Mura," Madame Fournier said, "I do not know when now she will get the husband she wants."

"How long," Rennert asked curiously, watching the cat, "do these spells last with her?"

She shrugged.

"One cannot tell, señor, one cannot tell. A week, perhaps. It is at its worst now. I must get her a husband before it comes again."

The beads tinkled gently into place as the cat withdrew her head.

Rennert looked at the doorway thoughtfully and said across the semi-darkness: "The crystal was broken when Miss Noon came to this room last night?"

"No," Rennert had the feeling that Madame was choosing her words with care, "it was broken later. Mura sleeps in this room, you know, and I always put the crystal away in my room back there." She gestured toward the curtain-covered doorway. "But last night I forgot to take it from the table after Miss Noon was here, and Mura broke it during the night."

"I see." Rennert moved toward the door. "I hope that you will be able to rest tonight."

"*Gracias, señor.*" She got to her feet with an effort.

After Rennert had closed the door he heard behind him the quick turning of the key in the lock.

He stood in the sala and watched Mandarich's broad back disappear into the dining room. He walked quickly, then, up the right staircase and passed through Riddle's room and the bath to the artist's quarters. From the top shelf of the wardrobe he took the bottle of cognac which Mandarich had replaced. He put in into the inner breast pocket of his coat and left as he had come.

He descended the stairs, went through the sala to the terrace, and down the steps to the level of the street. The soldier stood upright by the cobblestones, his eyes studying Rennert's approach.

"*Buenas tardes.*" In the sunset-stillness Rennert's greeting sounded strangely loud.

The soldier's reply was noncommittal.

"I should like to buy a bottle of cognac," Rennert said, fingering coins in his pocket. "Is it permitted to call a boy and send him down to a cantina?"

The soldier looked doubtfully at the ground.

"You do not have orders against it, do you?" Rennert asked.

"No," the Mexican admitted, then looked up into Rennert's face. "Very well, señor, it is permitted."

Half a block down the street three small boys were squatting upon the cobblestones, tossing rocks against an adobe wall with as much seriousness as if the practice constituted a part of the day's duties. Rennert's call met with an instant response, for to

the muchachos of Taxco every visiting americano is a potential
Croesus. In a moment they were standing eager-eyed before
him, their bare toes clutching the smooth stones as they ma-
neuvered for position.

"Go to the first cantina down on the plaza," Rennert said,
"and buy a bottle of cognac Hennessey, *como éste,*" he held before them the bottle which he had abstracted from Mandarich's
room.

"*Sí, señor!*" they chimed.

He gave ten pesos to the foremost of the group and said:
"When you bring me the cognac there will be for each of you
a *propina.*"

"*Un momentito, señor!*" They turned and ran down the cobblestones, their voices blended in low, excited chatter.

"When are you relieved?" Rennert turned to the soldier.

"At the sixes, señor."

Rennert extended the bottle.

"Give this," he said, "to Captain Pérez tonight—without fail.
Ask him to have it analyzed at the *botica.* I think that it can
be done without difficulty. If not, ask him to send it to Cuernavaca or Mexico City. It is very important."

The soldier took the bottle and regarded it uncertainly.

"You had better keep it hidden until you are relieved,"
Rennert said.

"Bueno." The Mexican thrust it under his blouse.

Rennert stood for a moment looking down the hillside,
watching the last rays of the sun illumine the dome of Santa
Prisca's church, whereon majolica letters proclaimed: *Gloria a
Dios en las Alturas.*" ("Glory to God on the Heights.") Here
the Santa herself had appeared, so one is told in Taxco, and
had detained the lightning bolts with one hand as with the
other she waved a palm leaf in blessing over the temple and the
people of the little city. That, too, had been at the beginning of
a rainy season, centuries ago. . . .

"The American lady who came this morning," Rennert
asked, "what did she want?"

The soldier had resumed his rigid posture and looked at him
sidewise.

"She wanted to see Madame Fournier." He spoke mechanically.

"Did she tell you why she wanted to see Madame?"

"She said that she wanted to have her read the crystal and tell her future."

"She was disappointed when you would not let her come up to the house?"

"Yes, señor, she was very disappointed."

Up the hill came the three muchachos, joined now by two others, who formed, it would appear, an unwelcome escort. The leader held a bottle gripped firmly in his hands. When they had come to a standstill he thrust the others back and approached Rennert, the bottle extended.

"*Aquí tiene Vd. el cognac, señor.*"

Rennert took it and put three twenty-centavos pieces in the boy's still outstretched palm.

"*Para tí y tus amigos.*"

"*Gracias, señor.*"

The three drew aside in excited colloquy, and Rennert was turning away when he noticed the two boys who had brought up the rear. They were standing in the middle of the street, regarding him pleadingly.

"*Qué hay?*" he asked them.

"We, too, helped in bringing the cognac," one of them said with a self-assured air.

"And how?" Rennert suppressed a smile.

The boy glanced quickly in the direction of the three who were dividing their spoils and lowered his voice.

"Those others are not honest, señor. We watched to see that they did not run away with your money."

Rennert laughed and drew two more coins from his pocket. As he did so he glanced down the hillside and saw an even smaller youngster running in their direction. On his oval Indian face was a look of desperate urgency. Rennert hastily thrust the coins into the hands of the two self-appointed guardians of his purchase and made his escape up the steps. Behind him he heard the frantic call of the newcomer.

In the sala he glanced through the doorway of the dining room and satisfied himself that Mandarich was still engaged upon his meal. In his own room he carefully poured out part of the cognac into a glass, then made his way to the artist's chamber on the other side of the house and placed upon the top shelf of the wardrobe the bottle of cognac which the boys had brought him. Before doing so he took care to wipe all fingerprints from the glass and to scratch off a corner of the label.

Downstairs, upon the terrace, he stood once more and watched the sun dying upon the tiles of Santa Prisca's temple. Far below the glistening dome the deep barrancas were in shadow. They were, Rennert thought, like dark currents that flowed about the house upon whose terrace he stood, leaving it a shell of beauty hiding dark things. The sight of the light-impregnated tiles was to him a relief from the certainty that soon the bottle of cognac upstairs would hold upon its sides the fingerprints of the murderer of Donald Shaul and Stephen Riddle. . . .

"Daydreaming?"

Rennert turned with a start. Crenshaw stood in the doorway, watching him with an amused smile upon his lips.

"To tell the truth," Rennert said, "I was."

Crenshaw walked across the terrace to his side and glanced quickly about him.

"I thought," he said in a low, unhurried voice, "that you might be interested in seeing this." He drew from his pocket an envelope and handed it to Rennert. "It came in this afternoon's mail."

Rennert looked at the envelope. It was addressed to Mr. George Crenshaw, in care of Madame Fournier's pension. In the upper left-hand corner were printed the words: "Office of the President, Riddle Refining Co., Tulsa, Oklahoma." Rennert opened the envelope and took from it a sheet of paper. He read it thoughtfully. It was dated from Tulsa, five days before.

DEAR MR. CRENSHAW [it ran]:

Yours of the 1st inst., to hand and contents noted.

Your report on the party in question is satisfactory, and I trust that you will continue your observations for a time.

Kindly remain in Taxco until further notice. Should party leave, follow her and notify me of new address.

It has come to my attention that Dr. R. L. Parkyn is residing for a while in Taxco, at, I believe, the same address as yours. He is conducting some archæological researches in the mountains near by and has asked me for financial assistance in his work. I refused him when he first approached me on the subject, but recent developments make it probable that I may be able to reconsider his request. Kindly give me a report as soon as possible on the man, his activities down there, and whether, in your opinion, they warrant my interest. Dr. Parkyn believes that there are extensive deposits of jade in the mountains near Taxco. If possible, ascertain from miners or geologists if there is such a possibility. This letter will be entirely confidential, and you will not mention my name to Parkyn.

Should any additional expense be incurred in this new investigation, kindly add to my account.

Sincerely,

Owen Riddle.

"I thought," Crenshaw said, "that you ought to see the letter. It was written, you will notice, before the old man's son left Tulsa."

"Yes," Rennert slowly refolded the sheet and slipped it into the envelope, "thank you."

"It offers," Crenshaw said, "a new possibility, doesn't it?"

"You mean?" Rennert studied his face.

Crenshaw's gaze did not waver.

"I happen to know that old man Riddle was going to set his son up in the architectural business as soon as he graduated from college. Then the young fool fell in love with this actress. The old man told him that if he didn't give her up he wouldn't get a cent of help from him. The young fellow's dead now, and his father will probably be more likely to spend his money on Parkyn's goose chase."

Rennert looked at him thoughtfully.

"Is it true," he asked, "that Owen Riddle lost a considerable quantity of money not long ago?"

"Yes, that's true."

"Then he might not feel able to spend money both on his son's business career and on explorations in Mexico?"

Crenshaw nodded.

"Sure, that's the idea." He thrust his hands into the pockets of his coat and stood with his shoulders slightly hunched forward. "I don't like to throw suspicion on anybody, but I thought you ought to know about this."

"Thanks," Rennert said again. "But if young Riddle were going to marry Miss Noon regardless of his father's opposition, this would in itself make the money available."

Crenshaw's eyes narrowed slightly.

"But she turned him down yesterday," he said out of the corner of his mouth.

"True," Rennert nodded, "she did. But this would mean that someone knew that fact."

"Perhaps," Crenshaw said significantly, "someone did."


# CHAPTER FIFTEEN

### XIPE

Rennert deliberately studied the man—his fresh clean-shaven skin, his hard blue eyes that looked out from beneath slightly bushy brows, the long smooth line of his jaw.

"Do you have any reason for your insinuation, Mr. Crenshaw?" he asked a bit coldly.

The other rattled keys in his pocket for a moment.

"No," he said, "I don't, but it seems to me a perfectly natural supposition, considering how gossip spreads among a bunch of people who live in the same house and don't have anything else to do but watch their neighbors."

"You're assuming, then, that Stephen Riddle was murdered."

Crenshaw drew a hand from his pocket and surveyed its nails. He said: "Sure. Aren't you?"

"I think it extremely probable," Rennert said, and handed him the letter.

"Very well," Crenshaw smiled slightly as he thrust it into a pocket of his coat. "What's the use of stalling, then?" He wheeled about and strode across the terrace to the door of the sala.

Rennert sat for a long time upon the balustrade, thinking. At last he got up and went into the house and up the stairs. At the door of Dr. Parkyn's room he knocked.

A gruff voice bade him enter.

He opened the door and stepped into the room. Parkyn was seated at a small deal table by the window, a mass of papers before him. He laid down the fountain pen which he had been using and turned in his chair.

"Come in," he said without enthusiasm, "and sit down."

"I'm interrupting, I see," Rennert said.

Parkyn took his pipe from the tray upon the table.

"I was on the point of quitting," he said as he picked up his pouch and shook tobacco into the bowl of the pipe. "It's getting too dark to write any more." He tossed the pouch to the table and got up. He walked across the room and switched on the light.

The room was filled with a variety of objects. Under the table, serving as a rest for the feet, was a small packing box, its partially pried-off lid revealing a quantity of coarse sacking. Ranged upon the table and the dresser were stone images, fragments of pottery, masks, and obsidian flakes.

Rennert sat in a chair over which a red-and-white-and-green Oaxaca *sarape* had been thrown.

Parkyn resumed his seat by the table and peered at him over the rim of his glasses.

"What kind of a visit is this?" he asked. "Official or unofficial?"

Rennert smiled.

"Call it professional. I'm in search of information." He took from his pocket the jade mask which he had obtained from Madame Fournier. "I should like some information about this mask."

Parkyn took the jade without much interest and examined it. He turned it over, then looked up at Rennert.

"A mask of Xipe," he said.

"Beyond the fact that Xipe was an Aztec deity associated, I believe, with flaying, I know nothing about him. And as to the purpose of that mask I know nothing at all."

The effect of the electric light on Parkyn's glasses gave his eyes again a glassy-dead stare.

"The mask served no particular purpose," he said, "it was merely a specialization of the representation of the entire body in an image."

"And about Xipe?"

"Xipe"—Parkyn drew upon his pipe and stared over its bowl at Rennert—"was, as you've said, the god of sacrifice by flaying. He was probably originally a maize god from Oaxaca, and the flaying of the victim was doubtless symbolic, representing the husking of the corn. His ceremonial name was 'night-drinker,' and at times of drought, when the rains were delayed, he was invoked to give moisture to the crops. It was then that the sacrifices were made to him. This mask represents his face. Upon the reverse," he turned the jade over, "you see a representation of his entire body. Notice the peculiar rattle-staff which he, like all the water and fertility deities, carried, and which was supposed to be a charm to bring rain by imitating its sound. Notice also the skin dress which he wears. It was this, probably, which caused Xipe to become associated with skin diseases——"

"With skin diseases?" Rennert was staring at the little piece of jade.

"Yes, those who were suffering from diseases of the skin were believed to be under the protection of Xipe and, if they died, to go to Tlacolan, the abode of the rain deities, in compensation, probably, for their sufferings upon earth. This is a particularly good example of Aztec jade carving but not exactly rare. Where did you get it?"

"It belonged to Madame Fournier and was stolen. She found it in the kitchen where she believes the cook hid it. I bought it from her and wondered if it had any value."

Parkyn's fingers were suddenly still upon the sides of the little figure. His eyes rose to meet Rennert's.

"The cook?" he repeated as if to himself. "Strange." He

thought a moment, then shrugged. "She probably thought it was a valuable piece that she could sell. All these Indians are obsessed by the idea that the little pieces of pre-Conquest stuff they pick up out in the mountains are extremely valuable."

He handed the mask back to Rennert. Rennert returned it to his pocket. He had the feeling that there was tension in the air. Parkyn seemed abstracted and kept staring into the bowl of his pipe.

"Did you find out," Rennert asked, "what Esteban meant by the word 'nagual'?"

Parkyn sat very still, as if held by the sight of the glowing tobacco.

"You will remember," Rennert said, "that you and I were talking about it this morning before you went to Riddle's room. You said something about going to find out if that is what the boy really said."

Parkyn began to raise and lower his fingers upon the arm of the chair.

"Oh, yes, of course," he said, "I had forgotten." He hesitated. "Well, I was unable to talk to him. But his case interests me."

"His illness?"

"No," Parkyn pursed his lips so that his mustache crept down on each side of his mouth, "not his illness so much as his use of the word 'nagual'—if that is what he really said."

"You've never told me what the word means."

Parkyn threw one leg over the other and settled himself in the chair.

"How well do you know Mexico?" he demanded.

"The more I live here the less I know about it," Rennert said frankly.

He saw an answering gleam of comprehension in the scientist's eyes.

"In that case," the latter said, "you will put more credence in what I'm going to tell you. I'll admit," he smiled slightly, "that it sounds a bit melodramatic."

Rennert waited.

"It really goes back to pre-Conquest Mexico, where the belief in the practice of the black arts was prevalent, as indeed it is today. More so, perhaps, than we realize." His voice took on a didactic tone: "In the time of the Aztecs the Naualli was a high priest who possessed magical powers, including those of levitation and the assumption of animal form at will. He acted as the general guardian of the city against sorcerers and gave warning of approaching famine or pestilence. After the Conquest by the Spaniards, the belief in such powers by certain individuals became very widespread and resulted in the formation of a regular cult, the members of which were called Nagual. They were believed to have animal familiars, whose shape they could assume, and to hold regular 'witches' sabbaths.' Under torture, many of the natives confessed to such practices and the Spaniards had great difficulty in stamping out the cult, which had for its avowed object the elimination of Christianity in Mexico." Parkyn leaned over and tapped the contents of his pipe into the tray. "An extremely interesting recrudescence of paganism," he said, his eyes intent on the operation.

"Do you mean," Rennert asked, "that such a belief may not have entirely died out?"

Parkyn was slowly refilling his pipe, spilling a great quantity of the tobacco in the process.

"Such beliefs disappear very slowly, particularly in a country like Mexico, with a large aboriginal population. And there have been reports in recent years that Nagualism as a cult is being revived. The Revolution, you know, gave a tremendous impetus to the regeneration of the native cultures. When you mentioned Esteban's use of the word, referring to the Siamese cat, I was interested, since it was the first authenticated instance I have been able to find of the present-day existence of the belief."

"I have lived in Mexico," Rennert said, "long enough to accept the possibility of the existence of any kind of belief."

"Yes," Parkyn nodded slowly, "the revival of all the forms of old worship, such as that of Quetzalcoatl, which D. H. Lawrence described in *The Plumed Serpent,* is of course absurd, but the basic idea is significant. I want to talk to Esteban as soon as possible and find out just what is on his mind—

if he really believes the cat is a human being, possibly an enemy of his, who has assumed animal form."

"That would account for the attempt to poison the cat."

"Yes, and the failure of the cat to eat the poison would add weight to the belief that she was a being possessed of supernatural powers."

"And the mask of Xipe?"

Parkyn shrugged and stared intently at the bowl of his pipe. Smoke rose upward in slow spirals, like incense.

"Might have been taken by the cook," Rennert went on, "in the belief that it would serve as a protection for the sick boy."

"Yes." Parkyn's voice sounded as if his thoughts were elsewhere. "That is entirely possible." He changed the subject abruptly. "Heard anything more about how long we are likely to be kept cooped up here?"

"No," Rennert said, "I haven't."

Parkyn sat for a moment, puffing savagely at his pipe.

"I hope," he said, "that we shall be able to get away soon. Personally, I'm running short on funds."

"You've given up hope of locating any of those jade deposits, then?"

"No, not given up hope, but it takes money—and several sources to which I'd looked for help failed me. Then, too, the rainy season is about to begin, so there won't be much chance for exploration for several months. I hope by next fall to be able to come back and accomplish something. I haven't been able to do much so far but reconnoiter." He looked up at Rennert over the rim of his glasses. "They're not likely to keep us here, after this quarantine business is over, on account of these two deaths, are they?"

"I think not."

"What did that Mexican officer learn about Riddle's death?"

"I told you," Rennert said, "that my visit here was unofficial. That was no prevarication. So I feel free to tell you that he has learned that you entered Riddle's room this noon instead of merely knocking at the door."

Parkyn's face, seen in the light of the unshaded electric bulb, looked fierce and hawklike in its sudden immobility. For a long time he did not speak, and his pipe made low gurgling noises as he drew upon it.

"Good God!" he exclaimed explosively, "he doesn't suspect that I—he doesn't think that I had any object in going in that room except to take the boy down to lunch, does he?"

"I don't know that he does, Dr. Parkyn. But you made a mistake by not adhering to the truth. I think," he added carefully, "that you had better tell me exactly what happened."

Parkyn took the pipe from his mouth and slowly ran his tongue over full red lips.

"Yes," he said, "I suppose it would be better. I saw no reason for implicating myself in something I wasn't at all concerned in, so I let it go at the fact that I knocked on the door. When I knocked, however, Riddle called to me to come in. I did so. He was sitting on the edge of the bed, writing a letter. He looked washed out and sick. He told me that he was going to go to sleep and asked me if we could postpone our conversation until later. I assured him that that would be all right with me and left the room." His gaze met Rennert's squarely. "That was all."

"Did you notice what was on his table?"

"A small pasteboard box, I believe, and a glass. And his writing material, of course."

"Exactly what did Riddle do while you were in the room?"

Parkyn thought a moment.

"He was just finishing the letter. He addressed an envelope, blotted it, and put the letter in it. Then he put it in the drawer of the table."

"He blotted it?" It was with an effort Rennert kept his voice steady.

Parkyn looked at him in some surprise.

"Why, yes, he blotted it."

"With what?"

"With what?" Parkyn stared at him. "Why, with a blotter, of course."

"Where was the blotter?"

"On the table."

"Did he put it in the drawer with the letter?"

"Really, I don't remember, but I believe that he did."

"Could you see whether there was another envelope in the drawer?"

"No, I was some distance away."

"I wonder," Rennert said, "if you would be able to identify the letter which Riddle was finishing when you entered?" He drew from his pocket the envelope which he had taken from Riddle's room, removed the letter, and handed both to Parkyn.

The latter took them in his hands and glanced at the inscription upon the envelope. Rennert, watching him closely, saw the muscles about his eyes contract a trifle.

"It looks like the same one, but I couldn't be positive." As he spoke, Parkyn's eyes were rapidly traveling over the penned lines upon the sheet of paper. When he had come to the end, he stared steadily at the paper, and Rennert thought that his fingers tightened slightly upon it. Distinctly noticeable was the gleam in his eyes as they rose slowly to meet Rennert's. "It doesn't seem from that," he said abstractedly as he handed the letter and envelope back to Rennert, "that Riddle intended to commit suicide, does it?"

"No," Rennert replaced them in his pocket, "it doesn't." Parkyn's immobile features had betrayed nothing, but he was positive that he had read surprise in the archæologist's eyes. Surprise and exultation that could be accounted for only by the man's knowledge that Riddle had stood between him and the attainment of his ends.

Rennert got to his feet. He experienced again that feeling of bafflement which he had felt so often in this affair at Madame Fournier's. There had been, he was positive, no blotter either upon the top of the table in Riddle's room or in the drawer.

Hastily excusing himself, he left Parkyn's room and returned to Riddle's. Another thorough search convinced him that he had not been wrong. There was no blotter in the room.

He sank into a chair and took from his pocket the letter which he had taken from the drawer. He reread it. He sat for a long time staring at the exotic yellow flowers and asking himself what messages both Shaul and Riddle could have written that would necessitate the removal of the blotters which had dried them. For if the letter which he held in his hands were the only one which Riddle had written, to have left the letter and removed the blotter were sheet madness.

And for the first time he asked himself if madness were the answer to this singularly baffling case.

## CHAPTER SIXTEEN

### THE BELLS OF SANTA PRISCA

R ENNERT WAS FINISHING a belated dinner when Dr. Otero came to the house. From where he sat he saw the young man enter the sala and arose hastily to intercept him. He drew him out upon the terrace and spoke in a low voice.

"Your instrument case was found this afternoon, doctor. It is in my room. Do you need it before you see Esteban?"

Otero's face looked paler and more ascetic than ever in the light from the head of the stairs.

"Many thanks, señor," he said, "I could not find it. I looked in all parts, but I could not find it. No, I do not need it when I see the sick boy."

"Suppose," Rennert said, "that you come to my room as soon as you are through with Esteban. I should like a few words with you."

"Very well, señor."

Rennert walked with him into the sala and made his way back to the dining room. He finished his coffee, lit a cigarette, and went up to his room.

He entered it and switched on the light, in which he had placed another bulb. He sensed at once that something was wrong and stood for a moment surveying the place. It was nothing tangible, nothing as tangible even as the faint scent which he thought—but was not sure—met his nostrils. But he was positive, as he stood there, that someone had been in that room but a few moments before.

His thoughts went at once to the lower drawer of the trunk. He stepped quickly across the room and opened it. The instrument case and the jade mask rested there, to all appearances undisturbed. He closed the drawer and went to the flat-topped table by the window. Two books lay upon its surface. He opened the drawer and took out its contents. Stationery and envelopes, a small memorandum book, two pencils . . .

He laid them back in the drawer and stared at them. He swore very softly under his breath. For nothing was missing, he was positive, except the small rectangular piece of blotting paper which had lain under the writing material.

He closed the drawer and sank into a chair. He tossed the end of his cigarette through the window and lit another. He was still sitting there, his head wreathed in smoke, when the doctor came. His knock coincided with the arrival in Rennert's mind of an explanation of the missing blotting paper. It fitted so well with an angle of the case which had been apparent from the beginning that he wondered it had not occurred to him sooner.

He got up and opened the door. He thought, as he motioned Otero to a chair, that he looked frightened. His eyes seemed to avoid Rennert's.

"How is the sick one?" Rennert asked as he sat down opposite him.

Otero shrugged his narrow shoulders and spread his bleached-looking hands palms outward in a gesture expressive of discouragement.

"He is worse, señor. The fever is higher, and the pain in his abdomen is increasing. He cannot eat and is delirious most of the time." His pale, fragil-looking fingers plucked at the cuff of his coat, and he added: "I think, señor, that he will die."

Rennert frowned.

"Has the rash upon his abdomen begun to spread?"

The Mexican's furtive black eyes flicked Rennert's face and rested upon the wall behind and to one side of him.

"No, señor, it has not spread."

"Then it must not be measles or smallpox? Wouldn't the rash have begun to spread by this time?"

"Yes, señor," there was reluctance in the voice, "it should be spreading now."

"If it is not measles or smallpox," Rennert pursued, "what,

in your opinion, could it be? I know nothing about medicine, but it strikes me there ought to be some alternative."

There was a worried look in the young man's eyes, and he shifted his position uneasily in the chair.

"But I am sure," he said with an emphasis oddly at variance with his manner, "that it is the measles. By tomorrow, yes, the rash will have spread. Dr. Pelaez will have returned then, and I am sure will tell me that I am right."

Rennert studied him thoughtfully for a moment.

"Esteban," he said, "was down in Terra Caliente not long ago, along the Balsas River. You have heard of the pinto?"

Otero's eyes were on Rennert's now and in them was a strange frightened look. They looked, the thought flashed across Rennert's mind, like those of a startled animal. Otero's smile, when it came, was a mere distortion of his thin lips.

"But yes, señor, I have heard them talk of the pinto. It is but another superstition of the ignorant ones—the Indians."

"Have you ever seen a case?"

"No, señor, never. I do not think there is such a disease. It is but another superstition of the ignorant ones."

Rennert got up and went to the trunk. He took out the instrument case and handed it to Otero.

"I wish that you would examine the contents of this case and tell me if there is anything missing."

The doctor took the case and opened it. Along the sides were holders for small bottles and, below them, a small assortment of scalpels, bandages, and scissors. Rennert stood and watched the doctor's white fingers as they went over the contents. Most of the bottles, he saw, were empty. He noticed the sudden tautening of the fingers as they paused at one of the holders.

Otero looked up at Rennert. The color had drained entirely from his face, so that his black hair and eyebrows stood out with ghastly prominence.

"Yes," he said, "there is something missing."

"What?" Rennert did not hide his interest.

"A bottle—a small bottle—of chloroform."

"That is all?"

"Yes, señor, that is all, but I do not understand who could have taken it."

Rennert stared thoughtfully at the contents of the case.

"What medicines or drugs do you keep in there?" he asked.

Otero smiled disarmingly, revealing his flashing white teeth. It was as if he were giving vent to his nervousness.

"But little, señor. A little chloroform and some purgatives. This case," he closed it carefully, "is really not necessary, you know, but these people here think that a doctor must carry one. They feel that it gives him importance."

"You carry no poisons or drugs in it, then?"

"No, señor, none."

"Very well," Rennert said, "many thanks for having come up here."

"Ah, señor, many thanks to you for finding the case."

"Don't thank me," Rennert said, "but Mrs. Giddings. She found it and gave it to me."

"Ah, yes, the Señora Giddings." The doctor had gotten to his feet and was again pulling down the cuffs of his coat. *"Es muy simpática*—I am sorry that I could not help her."

"Help her?"

"Yes, to get the drug—the veronal."

Rennert repeated very carefully: "The veronal?"

"Yes, the veronal. The Señora says that she cannot sleep and asked me to get the veronal for her. But, alas, I could not. Here in Taxco they do not sell such things."

"And when," Rennert tried to keep the interest out of his voice, "did the Señora Giddings ask you to get the veronal?"

"Yesterday, señor. She has been sitting up each night with Esteban and has not been able to sleep. It is too bad, but I do not know where she can get the veronal."

Rennert bid the doctor good-bye and sat for a long time, smoking and looking into the darkness.

Down in the plaza the band was playing a melancholy waltz whose endless repetitions were in tune with his thoughts. Down under the laurel trees, he knew, they were in the midst of the *paseo*—girls and men endlessly circling the plaza in opposite directions. In such never ending circles did his thoughts run.

The bells in the cathedral began to clang. Not the least diverting feature of life in Taxco is the personal equation which enters into the erratic ringing of the bells in the cathedral. As a means of determining the hour they are worthless; as an index of the sobriety or drunkenness, energy or lassitude of the bell ringer, they are invaluable. It sounded now as though the bell ringer were filled with an extraordinary amount of what *los norteamericanos* call "pep" or else were seized with remorse at his negligence. At any rate, they broke into the silence so sharply, so persistently, that they effectively jarred him from his thoughts.

He got up and stood for a moment at the window, listening to the echo of the iron clangor die away in the barrancas. And, as he stood there, he heard below him the frenzied cries of the Siamese cat. They hung for an instant in the still air, then faded, as had the sound of the cathedral bells, amid the rocks.

He turned and walked to the door. As he stepped out upon the balcony his attention was caught by the sound of voices and the flashing of lights down by the street. Several uniformed figures were grouped upon the stone steps.

Rennert went downstairs, crossed the terrace, and descended the steps.

Upon the ground, under a stunted coffee bush, lay the young soldier who had stood guard through the day. Another soldier sat upon the ground, impassively supporting his comrade's head, and, in the flickering illumination of the torches, Rennert caught a glimpse of the prone man's cruelly distorted features and glassy, staring eyes.

Crazily, the cathedral bells began again with renewed vigor. The bell ringer must be very, very drunk.

Captain Pérez stepped up to Rennert.

"This soldier," he spoke hurriedly, "is dead. He was found thus when the other came to relieve him. It is, I think, poison." He held forth an empty cognac bottle. "This was found beside him."

Rennert's face was grim as he said: "Come with me, Captain. I am afraid that I am to blame for what has happened."

He caught one glimpse of Captain Pérez's sharp black eyes

as he turned up the steps. His thoughts, as he led the way to his room, were not pleasant.

When he and the Captain sat in his room Rennert said: "As I told you, Captain, I am to blame for this soldier's death. I saw a bottle of cognac in one of the rooms here, I suspected that it contained poison—probably arsenic—and removed it. I gave it to that soldier to give to you when he was relieved. I wanted it analyzed in order to be sure. I should, however, have cautioned him not to drink it. That is doubtless what he did."

Pérez's manner had changed from the thinly veiled indifference he had manifested before. He was now alert and regarded Rennert with restless black eyes.

"And in whose room did you find this poison, Señor Rennert?"

"In that of Señor Mandarich."

He saw Pérez's fingers stiffen upon the arm of the chair and his lips tighten into cruel straight lines.

"This Mandarich," there was a silky quality about the voice, "we shall question him at once. Take me to his room."

They walked in silence down the stairs and up to the other wing. One thought was running now through Rennert's mind. It was: *Again the screaming of the cat has presaged death!* For he remembered the frenzied screaming that had come through the night air as he had stood at his window.

At the door of Mandarich's room he stood aside and said: "This is the room."

Pérez rapped sharply upon the wood. Almost instantly the door was thrown open, and Mandarich faced them. A look of surprise crossed his face as his eyes went from one of them to the other.

"Good-evening," he said, "come in." He stood aside rather awkwardly.

They entered, and Mandarich gestured toward chairs. They remained standing.

"Captain Pérez has instructed me to question you again, Mr. Mandarich," Rennert said.

"Again?" Mandarich eyed him speculatively.

"Yes. This afternoon you offered me a drink of cognac." He noticed the sudden narrowing of the other's eyes. "When I put it to my lips I suspected the presence of poison—arsenic, probably. As you remember, I did not drink it. Later I returned and removed the bottle from your wardrobe. I gave it to one of the soldiers, with instructions to have it analyzed. He, however, drank it. He is dead.'"

Mandarich stood for a moment, motionless, then moved uncertainly backward and sank onto the edge of the bed. He stared at Rennert. The enamel immobility of his face would, in other circumstances, have been comical.

"Naturally," Rennert said, "a statement from you is in order."

Still Mandarich sat with his large hands clasping his kneecaps. The tendons in his hands stood out like tautened wires.

"You're sure," his voice came unevenly, "that the cognac was poisoned?"

"The soldier is dead. An analysis will be necessary for definite proof."

Mandarich straightened himself upon the bed and threw back his shoulders. Color suddenly suffused his face.

"It was Riddle's cognac," he said with savage emphasis, "not mine! He gave me a bottle this morning, said that he was going to quit drinking, and he didn't want it around the room or he might be tempted to take some more. I didn't taste it." His eyes narrowed as he peered at Rennert through the glasses. "*I thought* you acted damn queer when I offered you that drink!"

Rennert turned to Pérez and summarized rapidly in Spanish his conversation with the artist. The Captain's eyes had the blackness and all of the sharpness of two obsidian flakes as he scrutinized Rennert's face.

"And do you think," he asked softly, "that he tells the truth?"

Rennert hesitated.

"I think," he said at last, "that he does. I certainly advised Riddle to slow down on the drinking." He turned to Mandarich and asked in English: "At what time did Riddle give you the bottle of cognac?"

"Just before noon, when he came back to his room."

Rennert nodded acquiescence.

"It would seem," he said to Pérez, "that such was the case.

And I'm sure that Mandarich *did* notice my action in refusing to drink the cognac. If he had been aware that it contained poison he would scarcely have been foolish enough to leave it about in his room after seeing that my suspicions were aroused. And," he added thoughtfully, "remember that we know of no reason why Mandarich should have wished to do away with either Riddle or Shaul."

Pérez's eyes ferreted into Rennert's face.

"Do you know anything about this man?" he asked. "Why he comes to Taxco?"

Rennert turned to Mandarich.

"The Captain," he said, "would like some information about you. Where you come from, what your purpose is in coming to Taxco, and so on."

Mandarich got up with alacrity and crossed the room to the dresser. He pulled open a drawer and fumbled among its contents, turning around finally with an envelope in his hand. He handed it to Rennert. "My passport," he said.

Rennert drew from the envelope the oblong card which serves visitors to Mexico for a brief period in lieu of a passport. It certified that Albert Martineau Mandarich, age forty-five, of New York City, an artist by profession, was the person whose bespectacled face stared forth from the small photograph pasted at one side. He handed it to Captain Pérez with the remark, "Everything seems in order."

"Yes," Pérez said hesitantly after a minute scrutiny of the card, "it seems so." He handed it back to the artist. To Rennert he said: "Let us leave this man unmolested—for the present," gently stressing the last word.

"Your explanation satisfies the captain," Rennert said to Mandarich. "Do you have any idea when poison could have been put into the cognac?"

"None at all." Mandarich shook his head emphatically.

"Where did Riddle keep the bottle?"

"On the dresser in his room, I think."

"Very well, then, Mandarich, we'll bid you good-night."

Mandarich sat for a moment in silence, as if he had not heard Rennert's words, then got heavily to his feet and crossed the room. As he held the door open for them he looked straight into Rennert's eyes and said: "A narrow escape, Mr. Rennert."

Rennert said: "Which goes to prove the truth of the adage about the cup and the lip, Mr. Mandarich," and stepped across the threshold.

## CHAPTER SEVENTEEN

### NEGOTIUM PERAMBULANS IN TENEBRIS

A BREEZE, DUST-LADEN, slid over the roof and played with the bronze lamp, so that the terrace below was a place of gently moving shadows as Rennert and Captain Pérez emerged from Mandarich's room.

"Señores!" a voice hailed them from the stairs.

They looked down to see Madame Fournier slowly ascending. Halfway up she paused and put both hands upon the railing. She leaned against it for a moment, breathing heavily, then continued her ascent. When she stood at the top her eyes went quickly from the Mexican to Rennert.

"Señores," her voice was labored, "what has happened? Those men at the foot of the steps—what are they doing?"

Rennert said evenly, before the Captain could reply: "They are removing a dead man."

"A dead man!" She stood stock still, both hands grasping the ends of the rebozo, and stared at him. "But who, Señor Rennert? What has happened?"

"It is one of my soldiers," Pérez began in voluble Spanish, "he has been poisoned——"

"I would suggest," Rennert said, "that we go to my room to talk." He led the way.

When he had closed the door behind them he motioned toward chairs and stood by the window.

"As Captain Pérez says, one of his soldiers, who stood guard today down by the street, has been poisoned. Arsenic, we think it was." He watched Madame Fournier.

"Arsenic?" Her stare was unreadable, and her fingers might

have been numb as she crossed herself mechanically. "You think that someone gave him arsenic?"

"Yes," Rennert interposed quickly, "that is what we suspect, although we have no proof as yet."

"Someone in this house?" Her black eyes shifted to Rennert's face.

"Yes, madame, in this house."

"You suspect Señor Mandarich?"

Rennert remembered that she had seen them come out of the artist's room. He said: "We questioned him, yes, but he convinced us of his innocence. We had been informed that he had in his room a bottle of cognac."

"And it was cognac which the soldier drank?"

"We believe so." Rennert was evasive.

Her old face was orderly, composed, but her thin lips were working as if forming unspoken words.

"Was arsenic kept about your house, madame?" Captain Pérez demanded with a trace of impatience.

Her gaze darted to his face. Her lids looked abnormally heavy, and whatever expression her eyes held was veiled. Both hands were buried now in the folds of the rebozo.

Pérez repeated his question, leaning forward in his chair.

She stared now at the floor and said in a toneless voice: "Señor Rennert knows."

"She is referring," Rennert told him, "to the rat poison which was taken from the kitchen and put into the food for the cat this morning." He regarded the woman thoughtfully. "Do you know," he asked her, "if all the arsenic was put in the tortillas or if some remained?"

She continued to stare at the floor, and Rennert thought that her stooped shoulders trembled a bit.

"I think, señor, that some remained."

"What did you do with the poisoned tortillas?"

"I burned them, señor, in the stove in the kitchen. I looked in all parts for the rest of the poison but could not find it."

"She thinks," Rennert said to Pérez, watching her, "that the cook took it to poison the cat."

There was a sudden convulsive movement of the woman's

face, as if the muscles beneath the sagging skin were tugging in vain at an inert mass.

"The cook?" Pérez spat out the question. "Why do you think she took it? You saw her?"

"No, *mi capitán,* but she took a mask from my room this morning, the room in which the poison was found. I know, then, that she was in there."

Captain Pérez was leaning forward, his eyes fixed on her face, and Rennert could sense the tenseness in his attitude.

"This cook," he demanded, "is named Micaela Guerrero, is she not?"

Madame Fournier's face had regained its impassivity and might have been a poorly wrought mask as she stared at the Captain. But deep in her eyes fear glinted.

"Yes," she said almost inaudibly, "she is Micaela Guerrero."

Captain Pérez got to his feet, his hands clenched at his sides.

"Why did you not tell me?" His voice was vibrant with anger. "All explains itself, then. I heard but a moment ago from one of the soldiers downstairs of the identity of this cook of yours." As he talked he strode to the door and threw it open. Upon the balcony Rennert could hear his voice calling out staccato orders.

In a moment he reëntered the room.

"That is all, madame," he said curtly. "We shall question this Micaela Guerrero."

Madame Fournier got to her feet and seemed about to say something but evidently changed her mind. She moved heavily to the door and left the room.

Rennert lit a cigarette.

"And now," he said to the pacing captain, "suppose you tell me about this redoubtable cook whom Madame has been harboring in her house."

Captain Pérez stood with his back to the window, so that his voice came indistinctly to Rennert's ears.

"She has a reputation among the ignorant ones of Taxco of being a curandera," he said. "She sells charms to the ignorant ones, to the indios, charms to drive off the evil spirits. To the young ones of Taxco she sells love potions. She has much in-

fluence among them. These things, as you know, Señor Rennert, we do not allow, but," he shrugged helplessly, "what
can we do? The ones who go to her will not talk, they have
fear of her. A year ago she was arrested, when the father of
one of the young men of the town made complaint against
her. She had sold the sweetheart of his son a magic drink to
enable the girl to win his love. The girl gave it to the young
man, and he became insane. He is now in an asylum at the
capital. We questioned this Micaela Guerrero, but we could
prove nothing. She said that she had given the girl nothing,
and the girl would not testify against her—for fear of her.
And so we had to let her go. We warned her, however, and
told her that the next time she did such things she would go
to prison. One or two times we have suspected that she was
in her business again, but we had no proof. Now"—he wheeled
about and faced Rennert—"she shall be arrested."

Rennert regarded him thoughtfully.

"But, granted that she once drove a man insane with her
potions, why would she wish to use arsenic on one of the
guests here? On this young Riddle in particular? Because," he
added, "the arsenic was evidently put in the cognac intended
for him."

Pérez kept eying the door expectantly.

"Such a one," he exclaimed, "who knows what she would
do?" His eyes glittered in the dim light. "She may have been
paid to do it. If so, we shall force her to talk." He moved to
the door and opened it. He stood for a moment upon the
threshold peering out, then walked down the balcony. Through
the half-open door Rennert could hear the sound of voices
below.

It was a long time before the Captain returned. His step
was quick, and anger thickened his dark face.

"She is gone," he said at the door, "she is not in the house!
She will have made her escape while the steps to the street
were unguarded!"

Rennert got to his feet. The announcement had taken him
by surprise. Could it be, he was asking himself, that he was
mistaken in his growing certainty as to who was responsible
for these deaths?

"I have given orders for her to be traced," the Captain said.
"We shall find her soon." He turned toward the door.

"By the way," Rennert asked, "you saw the contents of the
pockets of both Shaul and Riddle, did you not?"

"Yes." Pérez paused.

"Was there in the pockets of either of them a letter, a note,
a single piece of paper, upon which anything had been written in ink?"

"No, señor, there was nothing which had been written in
ink." The Captain stood for a moment, an unspoken question
in his eyes, then with a shrug turned down the balcony. He
left Rennert staring thoughtfully at the blackness framed by
the open door.

The momentary breeze had died, leaving only particles of
dust in the hot air. Clouds banked the western horizon. They
lay, these clouds, upon the tops of the mountains like black
eruptions from volcanoes, pregnant with menace.

Rennert walked down to the terrace and gazed into the sky
above the projecting roofs. His restiveness persisted, intensified
now by the advent of darkness. He began to walk up and down
the tiles, thinking about the case. On the surface it looked so
simple, now that some of the bothersome details were beginning to straighten themselves out in his mind. That remark
of Riddle's, for instance. Rennert understood it now. And he
knew who had removed the pillowcase from Shaul's room. He
catalogued in their places the manuscript which he had found
in Shaul's trunk, the blotting papers abstracted from the various
rooms, the poisoned cognac, the bruise upon Gwendolyn
Noon's elbow, Madame Fournier's shattered crystal. And yet
(he felt in his pocket for a cigarette) did everything dovetail
so nicely together? There was the flight of the cook, who he
felt sure had purloined the idol from Madame Fournier's room.
And the sickness of Esteban. Was there some other force at
work in the house, some force whose workings were too
devious for his straight-thinking mind to follow?

In one of the Psalms there was a phrase that had always
stuck in Rennert's mind, it so well epitomized the fears that
mankind had always had of the outer darkness, of the unknown things that lurk there—unguessed at by the ordinary

individual until he wakes at three in the morning and finds all the world at rest save his mind, superactive. *Negotium perambulans in tenebris. The pestilence that walketh in darkness,* the psalmist is translated. But Rennert had known once an individual in a city near his college town who had had other ideas about the psalmist's meaning. He was an old man, an unfrocked minister of the Gospel of whom many things were whispered in the little Midwestern community. He read the Hebrew of the Old Testament and the Arabic of the Koran. By some accident Rennert had become acquainted with him and would occasionally seek him out, fascinated in spite of himself by the old man's vehement discourses on human shortcomings. The "negotium" which walks in the darkness, according to him, had been rendered "pestilence" by a translator who feared to put down on paper what was really meant. The "negotium," he would say in a voice that took on the ardor of fanaticism, was the essence of mankind's fears, the menace which is the more terrifying because sensed rather than seen, and rendered corporeal by devil inventors who realized that a known evil was less to be dreaded than an unknown one. "When you grow older," the old man had told him once, peering into his eyes through thick-lensed glasses, "you will wake sometimes at three in the morning and strain your ears for some sound, something to tell you that your fellow beings are about you. There will be no sound, and the darkness will shut you in. Misgivings, denied during the waking hours, will return increased in magnitude. If you are one of those unhappy beings who have imagination you will have a drug handy to bring you oblivion, or else you will turn on the bed light and read your mind into submission. Then, if ever, you will be tempted to commit suicide. For then—and only then—all the flimsy screens which man has built up between himself and the terrors which he denies are down and he can stare beyond . . ."

"You, too, are unable to sleep tonight?" a voice said behind him.

Rennert laughed at his start. He had not realized how his thoughts had carried him away from his moorings.

"Yes," he said, recognizing Mrs. Giddings. "I just had a strange thought—that I couldn't rest until the rains come."

She walked toward him across the tiles, her soles noiseless upon their polished surfaces. Deep in the clouds lightning flashed.

"They must surely be close at hand now." She leaned upon the railing and stared up at the sky. "I never knew it to be so hot and close in Taxco. There's not a breath of air."

The light from the head of the stairs fell across the tiles, cutting her face in profile, so that it looked haggard, emaciated.

"Esteban is sleeping?" Rennert asked.

"Yes," she said abstractedly, "he's sleeping. I've given him a sedative."

"You should get some rest yourself, then." Rennert studied her face.

She laughed.

"I've given up hope of resting until I'm too tired to keep going. Even the coming of the rain, I'm afraid, won't help me."

"There are drugs to make one sleep," Rennert said carefully.

She glanced at him quickly, and her fingers tightened upon the balustrade.

"Yes," she said after a moment, "I know about them." Her voice sounded curiously remote and had in it more than a trace of bitterness.

"I've taken them sometimes—veronal, for instance." Rennert was deliberately confidential. "It always brings sleep."

"Yes," she said slowly, "I know it does. I'm tempted myself sometimes. The other day I would have taken some if I could have gotten it. Luckily, I couldn't. It's my fear that keeps me from any kind of drugs."

"I judge you've had experience with them."

For a long time she did not speak but stood with her eyes fixed upon the sky.

With startling suddenness the electric lights were extinguished throughout Taxco, and darkness engulfed them.

She laughed self-consciously.

"I know that's going to happen every night, yet it always frightens me. It's as if something were rushing at you."

Rennert drew a cigarette from his pocket and lit a match.

He saw her eyes fixed upon its diminutive flame.

"To reassure us that all the light has not gone from the world," he said with a laugh. He drew upon the cigarette and flipped the match over the balustrade. It cut a wide spiral through the darkness and expired before touching the stones.

"A short-lived mission, that of the match," she said.

"Yes."

Silence fell between them again.

"You must be careful." The woman spoke with sudden surprising intensity.

"Careful?"

"Of course, yes." Her voice was strained. "I know what I'm talking about. It is so easy to begin, everyone thinks that *he* will not become a slave. He thinks that—until it's too late." She paused, and when she resumed her voice was again matter-of-fact, conversational. "Back in the States," she said, "my husband is in a sanatorium. They think that they took him in time and that he can be cured. He began like that—afraid of lying awake in the early morning hours. The hours of despair, he used to call them."

"He must have had imagination."

"Yes," she agreed with a note of surprise, "that was the trouble. And now he's just a dead weight, a nonentity, while the best years of his life are going by. I tried to stay near him but could do nothing for him, so I came to Taxco. I thought that its impersonal beauty would make the waiting easier."

"And has it?"

"No." She paused as if to formulate her thoughts. "There's something about so much beauty, about such absolute perfection of beauty, that becomes unendurable after a while. That's why I've been taking care of Esteban. It has been something to keep me from thinking. About him—and the things we'd planned to do some day. How we'd spend a summer in Mexico sometime." Her voice sounded hollow. "But when summer comes most of the things one planned in the spring never come true." She paused. "There's that cat again!" It was almost a cry that escaped her.

The screaming seemed now to fill the house, gaining in intensity as it was echoed back by the walls. It came, Rennert could tell, from the sala and sounded as if the cat were approaching them.

"Mura must be loose," Mrs. Giddings said, with an effort to bring her voice under control.

They both looked at the doorway. The cat's body was invisible in the darkness, but her eyes were there, like two oval slits in a dark canvas masking glowing coals. She was silent now, her eyes fixed on them.

There was a low sound, more a moan than a cry, and something crashed in the dark room behind her. For an instant the eyes of the cat were averted, staring backward. Rennert, with sudden misgiving, started forward and saw the cat's eyes upon himself again. As he advanced, they retreated. Suddenly they disappeared as if snuffed out in the darkness, and Rennert stood in the doorway, gazing about the unrelieved darkness of the sala. Then he struck a match and stepped forward. As he did so the cat slowly backed away. Her angry growls might have been those of a small dog. When he gained the threshold of the outer door of Madame's chambers the cat had disappeared within. He could hear her crying again, lower now and with a plaintive note.

"What's happened?" Mrs. Giddings spoke at his shoulder. "Where is Madame Fournier?"

"Suppose we see," Rennert answered. "That's her bedroom beyond, isn't it?"

"Yes."

Rennert walked to the little table in the corner and applied the match to the wick of the candle which was stuck in a black Oaxaca jar. He held it up, surveying the room.

It had been ransacked. The curios in the cabinet were scattered about the shelves, and several of the masks lay upon the floor. A drawer of the table stood open. Its contents looked as if they had been frantically pawed over. Several playing cards were strewn over the tiles.

Rennert walked hastily to the door of the other room and rapped sharply upon the side. There was no response.

He stood in the doorway and held the candle aloft. Its flame was very steady in the still air and cast a feeble illumination over the long, low-ceilinged room. Against the opposite wall

was a huge bed with brass posts that glinted in the light. In the
bed lay Madame Fournier. Only her chin and a fringe of hair
that strayed from beneath a lace nightcap were visible, for a
white cloth covered her nose and mouth, masking her features.
The hand which hung over the side of the bed was motionless,
its fingers contracted into claw-like rigidity.

For the first time, Rennert heard Mrs. Giddings scream.

## CHAPTER EIGHTEEN

### UP THOSE STAIRS

Rennert's nostrils contracted as he bent over the bed and
jerked the cloth, a blue-monogrammed towel, from Madame
Fournier's face. He set the candle upon a chair and knelt upon
the tile.

"Is she—dead?" Mrs. Giddings's voice came faintly to his
ears.

"No, merely chloroformed, I think."

"Maybe I can do something for her."

Rennert got up and lit another candle, which stood upon the
dresser. As Mrs. Giddings busied herself at the bed he gazed
about the room.

His eyes rested in turn upon the silken Chinese shawls
draped about a long mirror on a marble-topped console, the
frayed fiber carpet that covered the tiled floor, the rotogravure
pictures pasted upon the whitewashed walls. They did not miss
the open drawers of the console and of the huge wardrobe,
nor the disarranged clothing that hung in the small closet in
the corner. It was evident that this room, like the anteroom
through which he had passed, had been subjected to a hasty
and frantic search.

His gaze came back to Mrs. Giddings, standing by the bed
and looking down at the inert figure therein.

"She'll be all right now, I think," she said, "but it's a good
thing we found her when we did. If she had remained the

rest of the night with that chloroform over her face . . . " She shrugged expressively.

Rennert was watching the Siamese cat, who crouched in the shadows under the bed and glared at him.

"You'll stay with her until she regains consciousness?"

"Yes, Esteban will not need me for a while."

"And you will call me as soon as she is able to talk?"

"Surely. She will be terribly sick, though, when she *does* recover. You'll probably have to wait until morning." She turned slowly and looked straight into his eyes. "I understand, of course, your wish to talk to her as soon as possible. You think that she will be able to tell you who—" for a barely perceptible instant she faltered—"who has been doing these things?"

"Perhaps, though she may have been asleep when she was chloroformed."

"Oh!" it was expressionless, "in that case you may know no more than you do now."

"No," Rennert said evenly, "I may know no more than I do now."

As he walked through the séance room, Mrs. Giddings followed him.

"I'll lock the door after you," she said with a lightness that did not deceive him. "It will be safer."

"And if you have to leave the room for any reason, be very sure that you lock the door."

As he stepped out into the dark sala he heard the key grate in the lock behind him.

Candle in hand, he walked across the room toward the stairs that led upward to the west wing. A foot from the lower tread he stopped at sight of the small still figure upon the tiles by the door that led to the quarters where Esteban lay.

It was María, the *criada* of Madame Fournier's establishment.

One brown forearm and hand lay darkly upon her crumpled white dress; the other, outstretched, still grasped a brass holder in which was fixed an unlighted candle.

Upon a low table beside the stairs stood a bowl of white *florefundio* bells. He tossed the flowers to the floor and carried the bowl to where the girl lay. He dashed water into her face and saw the startled return of consciousness. She lay for a moment, staring at him with wide-opened eyes that looked glassy against the light of the candle, then raised herself upon one elbow and looked into the darkness of the sala. Her face was gray-white.

"*Que te pasó?*" Rennert asked softly.

Her eyes came back to his face but she did not speak.

"*Algo te espantó?*" he went on.

"*Sí, señor,*" she whispered, sitting up now upon the tiles.

"And what was it that frightened you?" Rennert kept his eyes upon her face.

"Up those stairs it went." She seemed to have lost awareness of him and stared upward. "The *cura* in the church and the schoolmaster down on the plaza, they tell me that such things are not, that I but dream them. But I know, I have seen now——"

Rennert waited for her to continue, and when she did not, prompted: "You have seen what?"

He saw his mistake, for visibly her features tightened and she said: "*Nada, señor, nada.* I have seen nothing." She got to her feet, stood for a moment in indecision, then darted like a frightened animal toward the door of the dining room. Her bare feet seemed barely to touch the tiles.

Rennert watched her go then entered the room in front of which the girl had fainted. It was a small bare room with whitewashed walls. Crates and boxes stamped with the names of Mexico City stores were ranged along one side. Against the other wall was a small iron cot, and upon it Esteban lay.

It was the first time Rennert had seen the boy since the summer before, and the thought came to him that he would not have recognized the small tortured face as that of the genial smiling youngster who had once waited upon him with such evident pleasure. Esteban was sleeping, his breath coming and going almost imperceptibly.

Almost before he knew it, Rennert's gaze had left Esteban's face and was resting upon the yellow flowers in the unglazed pottery jar that stood upon an upturned box near the head of the cot. In the uncertain light of the candle their petals seemed to fuse into a mass of warm soft gold. *They symbolize,* he

thought, *the calm acceptance of the inevitable that underlies
the Mexican burlesque of death and makes the exit from this
life at once magnificent and horrible.* For he knew whoever
had placed those yellow flowers at Esteban's bedside was aware
of and had accepted the fact that Esteban was going to die.

He repressed the frantic feeling of impotence that suddenly
assailed him—in the United States one could busy oneself with
physicians, nurses, hospitals, druggists, but this was Mexico—
and walked on tiptoe out of the room.

He went up the stairs and paused upon the landing before
the thin pencil of light under Gwendolyn Noon's door. He
looked at it thoughtfully for a time before he knocked. For at
least sixty seconds he stood there before the door was thrown
open.

Gwendolyn Noon was a sharply done drawing in black and
white as she stood in the doorway, one hand upon the knob
and the other thrown stiffly across her jet-black cloak.

"Rather late for a call," Rennert said, "but I saw your light
and thought I'd risk an intrusion."

Her face was white and mask-like in the light of the candle
which he held; its flame dilated her eyes until they seemed
large and staring.

"Come in," she said in a husky voice, as she stepped to
one side.

Rennert crossed the threshold and watched her close the
door. She stood with her back to it and continued to stare
at him.

"What do you want?" she asked in the same voice.

"I'm sorry I was not in when you came to my room," he
said conversationally. "I thought I'd call and see if I could be
of any assistance to you."

Her eyes drilled into his face. She still held her right hand
thrown across the front of the black cloak so that the loose
sleeve fell away, revealing her forearm and elbow. Rennert's
eyes rested momentarily upon the damp edge of the sleeve and
the ugly purplish bruise upon her elbow (there was no mis-
taking it now). As if conscious of his scrutiny she quickly let
her hand fall to her side and her fingers clenched themselves
with a febrile movement. Their crimson nails seemed to be

digging into the white skin. *Curiously,* he thought, *like the painted claws of a cat.*

"To your room," she faltered. "Why, I——"

"I was told that you had called," Rennert said with careful emphasis. "It must have been while I was at dinner. I'm sorry."

She laughed—too loudly—and moved a few steps in the direction of the east wall.

"I had forgotten," she said, "it was nothing, nothing at all. I just wanted to—to apologize for losing my temper while I was talking to you and that Mexican officer this afternoon."

"Was that all, Miss Noon?" Rennert was looking past her into the mirror that stood upon the low console. Reflected in it he saw the marble slab which formed the top and lying upon it a glass of what looked like water, a half-empty bottle, and several sheets of blotting paper.

Suddenly her eyes narrowed, as if conscious of his scrutiny, and she stepped backward until her body concealed the top of the console. Her hands were held behind her.

"Yes," she said, "that was all. Why else should I have gone there?" Her laugh again was unnatural.

"I thought," Rennert said, "that you might have been looking for blotting paper."

"For blotting paper?" She seemed to force the words from her lips. "What an idea!"

"Because, Miss Noon, I understand why you took the blotting paper from Shaul's and Riddle's rooms, and I have read the story that is in that paper behind you now."

"You've read it?" She stared at him blankly for a moment before her eyes grew sharply speculative. Then they were calculative, and she was saying very distinctly: "How did you know?"

"Really, Miss Noon, there was only one explanation, after one looked beyond the apparent one that writing had been dried with the paper."

In her wide-open twitching eyes he read confirmation of all that he had suspected. He said: "Madame Fournier was chloroformed tonight. Fortunately she was discovered before she died. Otherwise there would have been another murder to add to the list of those which have occurred in this house. I doubt

whether she was able to recognize her assailant. Still," he held
out his hand, "I think that you are foolish to leave that bottle
of chloroform lying about. It provides too great a temptation—
and the next time its use might be fatal."

Incredibly, her white face seemed to have grown whiter. It
had lost, however, its mask-like appearance and was beginning
to twitch, as if she had lost the power to control her muscles.
Her hands moved, and Rennert saw that the right was now
in the pocket of her cloak.

"It is for your own salvation," Rennert said, thinking quickly
at the realization of what the movement probably meant. This
he hadn't expected. He still held his hand outstretched, but he
moved forward slightly. "Murder is contagious when one has
the example set."

Her eyes stared steadily into his, and she said with lethal
clearness:

"Why do you want that bottle?"

"I am going to return it to its owner," Rennert answered
quietly. His senses were alert now at the realization of his
danger, and he wanted to glance behind her.

Her eyes narrowed until they were mere slits.

"It's a trap," she said in a hoarse strained voice. The light
from the guttering candle upon the dresser glinted quickly
against the barrel of the small pearl-handled revolver which
she held now in her hand. The revolver was aimed directly
at Rennert's breast.

He stood very still and looked into her death-like face.

She held the bottle in her left hand now and was moving
very slowly toward the window. The revolver trembled, and
with a quick movement she tossed the bottle behind her. Glass
tinkled upon the stones far below.

Rennert smiled and said nothing, but his eyes watched the
finger that rested upon the trigger. He was thinking: *All
human values, life even, are sublimated to her one desire that
is becoming unendurable. If she believes that I stand between
her and that desire, no power on earth can keep that finger
from pressing the trigger.*

"Damn you!" Her voice took on a subtle change. It was no
longer deep and soft and musical, but coarse and slightly shrill.

Fury blazed in her eyes. "You have been interfering ever since you came here. What business is it of yours?"

He saw the look in her eyes change from one of anger to cold resolve and glanced at last past her.

"I think, Miss Noon, that in your case I should have chosen the frying pan," he said quietly as Mrs. Giddings stepped forward and quickly seized in her fragile-looking yet capable hands the wrist of the hand that held the revolver.

# CHAPTER NINETEEN

### MUSIC IN THE NIGHT

GWENDOLYN NOON's fingers went suddenly limp and offered no resistance as Mrs. Giddings drew the revolver from them. Her hand fell helplessly to her side, and she stood and stared dazedly at Rennert as he took the gun from the other woman and slipped it into his pocket.

"You made the mistake," he said quietly, "of thinking that I was constituting myself your judge. Such was not my intention."

Slowly her eyes went to the marble top of the console.

"You won't take it away from me, then?" she asked in a low tremulous voice.

"The blotting paper?"

She nodded almost imperceptibly.

"No," Rennert said, "I've already read the story in it."

"You've read it?" She moved with uncertain steps toward the bed and grasped one of the posts for support.

"It wasn't," Rennert said, "a very pleasant story."

He glanced at Mrs. Giddings, who had moved to the door that led to the connecting bathroom and was standing with her gaze fixed upon the tiles. She looked up and met his eyes. With a slight inclination of the head she turned and walked from the room.

"And now," Miss Noon said slowly when the door had closed, "tell me what you read in the blotting paper."

"I read an unpleasant yet rather pitiful story, one that is all too familiar to me. I read the story of a woman who wakes at three in the morning and sees phantoms staring at her out of the darkness, who is afraid to turn on the light and dispel them and who began by seeking a way to keep her eyes closed until daylight. Each time daylight was slower in coming, and the way she found to hasten it seemed always more necessary. Now she sees the phantoms about her even in the sunlight."

She did not speak, but in her staring eyes he read confirmation of his words.

He left her, still standing there, and walked out into the night. All at once words seemed futile against human frailty, and he guessed at what torture they constituted for her.

The night was still except for far-away thunder that rumbled in the mountains in the direction of the Huitzteco. Faint yet unmistakable in the nostrils was the smell of moisture. The rains, Rennert thought, must surely be at hand.

He undressed and sat for a long time at his window, smoking. He was in a strangely introspective mood. His words to Miss Noon had aroused forgotten responsive chords in his memory. In middle age an active and not unsuccessful life had already dulled most of the frantic urges toward more or less clearly defined ideals that used to assail him. Life to him was now a fairly leisurely affair that one surveyed objectively only at rare intervals and then in a more or less offhand fashion. Could it be, he was asking himself, that he had gained peace of spirit at too great a cost, complacency at the expense of dreams that once seemed bright?

Down in the street toward the plaza someone—probably the old *papaya* vendor who would produce a guitar and attempt "Sonny Boy" when tourists thronged the square—was singing in a low, monotonous undertone. The words came indistinctly to Rennert's ears, but he knew them only too well. There were no tourists upon the plaza now, and the old fellow was singing, for himself probably, a song of his people:

*"Jesu Cristo se ha perdido,*
*Su madre lo anda buscando."*

Rennert remembered him as he had looked the previous year, sitting upon the cobblestones and singing with his placid old face upturned to the sky. He had always reminded Rennert of an image of Tlaloc, the deity of the rains, hewn from dark stone by a long-dead hand.

> *"Donde me han visto*
> *Una estrella relumbrando?"*

he was singing. Much, Rennert thought, as he must have been singing that night when Donald Shaul sat in the cantina, smoking marihuana and listening to him. Rennert thought of the columnist's words, scribbled as the fumes of the weed crept upward into his brain, assorting so acutely sensations in pleasant and dread relief.

> *"Caminemos, caminemos,*
> *Hasta llegar al Calvario,*
> *Y por más que caminemos,*
> *Ya lo habrán crucificado."*

Rennert got up and tossed his cigarette from the window. Why, of all the songs in his repertoire, must the old fellow choose that particular one to sing at this time? The tragedy of Calvary and the questing Mother. . . .

> *"Let us hasten, let us hasten*
> *On to Calvary.*
> *But however fast we hasten there,*
> *They will have Him crucified."*

An *alabado* of Catholic Spain strained through the dark volcanic soil of Mexico to emerge the supreme expression of human futility, the *vacilada*. . . . Rennert blew out his candle and slipped between the sheets. Weariness swept over him in a flood, and he was soon in the delicious borderland of sleep. So deeply had a certain idea fixed itself in his subconscious that he did not realize at first, when he found himself sitting up in bed, what it was that had startled him. It was the echo that told him. In the stillness of the night the cries of the Siamese cat had carried a strangely childlike note, as of utter despair.

Rennert sat for a moment upon the edge of the bed, thinking. This was, he knew now, no fantastic imagining of his. For death had crept before along those quiet balconies outside, presaged by the cries of the cat.

He got up and walked to the door. He surveyed by the light of the candle the ineffective old lock, then carefully adjusted a chair beneath the handle.

Even when he had retired again, he lay for a long time, listening for a soft step upon the tiles. . . .

Rennert awoke early and lay for a time staring absently at the crests of the mountains, pink with sunlight. He must have dozed off again, for his next sensation was of irritation at the repeated tappings at his door. He got up, threw on a dressing gown, and opened it.

Captain Pérez stood upon the balcony.

His eyes were dull from lack of sleep, and lines creased his forehead. Rennert invited him in and sank upon the bed as he lit a cigarette.

"What's the news?" he asked.

The Mexican's agitation was manifest in his abstracted manner, his monotonous pacing of the floor, his absorption in the mountains visible through the window.

"Of this cook—this Micaela Guerrero—there is no trace," he said as he strode up and down the room. "We have searched for her throughout the night. She is not in Taxco, we are sure. That means that she has escaped to the mountains. Out there," he paused by the window and gestured helplessly, "we can never find her. She will dwell out there, in a cave, perhaps, and continue to use her influence over the ignorant ones of Taxco."

Rennert watched him over the curling smoke of his cigarette.

"You have fear, Captain. It is of that influence?"

Pérez stood still and stared out into the mountains.

"Yes," he said at last, his voice far away. "I have fear that she may bear an enmity for us of Taxco."

"But surely," Rennert laughed reassuringly, "you don't fear witchcraft, mud images stuck full of pins."

"No," the Mexican hesitated, "but there are other ways. This morning," he kept — carefully, Rennert thought — his face averted, "I went into a cantina down on the plaza for a glass of tequila. I had little rest last night, and this morning there was the matter of the americana at the Hotel Borda. The tequila tasted to me peculiar, and I did not drink it. I remembered last night."

"But the cognac which your soldier drank was not meant for him."

"True—" the Captain hesitated again—"but the keeper of this cantina, old Miguel, is said to have gone many times to this Micaela Guerrero in other days. If he should be still under her influence . . ." He left the sentence unfinished.

Silence fell between them, while outside the sun began to bathe the stony hills in warmth and to paint in pastel shades the diminutive houses of Taxco.

"You mentioned," Rennert said, "the matter of an americana at the Hotel Borda. What was that?"

Pérez's face looked in profile like finely flaked obsidian.

"Her name I do not remember. It is one of your names with many consonants. This morning, in the early hours, she fell from the balcony outside her window. Her skull was fractured upon the rocks. The mozo found her there just before the sun rose. They say that she must have been waiting for its rising. These things," he shrugged, "are bad for Taxco; they make the foreigners afraid to come here."

Rennert was immediately alert: "There is more, señor, than you have told me. What is it?"

Captain Pérez did not reply for several moments, but stood with his hands thrust into the side pockets of his uniform.

"It is," he said at last and with a trace of reluctance, "that the railing of the balcony is high—very high—and the americana could not have fallen off had she not climbed to the top. And why," he turned slowly to face Rennert, "should a person —even an americana—do that?" His manner implied a great deal about his opinion of americanas.

Rennert said thoughtfully: "For only one reason, Captain Pérez." Their eyes met. "Only if such a one wished to commit suicide."

The Mexican's eyes had lost some of their dullness now, and Rennert had the curious impression that a slow shifting was about to take place in their glassy blackness. His hands moved outward in a gesture of agreement.

"But surely," Rennert went on, "you are not connecting this Micaela Guerrero with the death of this woman?"

"I do not know, Señor Rennert. Even that is possible."

"But, granted that she could have accomplished it, what motive would she have had? Surely she could find other, easier ways to embarrass the authorities of Taxco, if that is her wish."

Pérez's fingers were gray and fragile-looking as they caressed the sides of a cigarette.

"Even that I can answer, señor." He struck a match and stared into its flame. "Her son"—he drew upon the cigarette and emitted smoke through his nostrils—"was a soldier in the Mexican army, a *pelado* conscripted from some pueblo north of here. He was killed by the americanos in 1917, during the" —Rennert could sense delicacy creeping into his manner— "regrettable occupation of Vera Cruz. It is said that Micaela swore then eternal hatred toward all your countrymen." He paused and seemed absorbed in contemplation of his cigarette. Its pungent odor was strong in the room. "And the poison," he concluded, "was put into the cognac of the young americano who died here. My soldier, as you say, but drank it by mistake."

Rennert thought: *Beneath his polished exterior lies a mind which is as abject a servant of superstition as that of any untutored Indian out in the mountains. Often, in the mestizo, it is more so, because its manifestations are relegated to the background of his behavior by fear of ridicule by the other world, of which he wants to form a part. He would prefer to believe this fantastic tale of witchcraft rather than the more terrible yet rational theory which has formed in my mind.* He wanted a cup of coffee to clear his thoughts.

Captain Pérez was studying his face.

"You do not agree with me, Señor Rennert, about this woman down at the Hotel Borda? You do not think that her death is connected with these others?"

"On the contrary, I believe that it is closely connected, that it all forms, as it were, part of a pattern."

The Mexican looked surprised.

"I thought, from your manner, that you did not agree." He seemed reassured. "We shall continue our search for Guerrero, then, since you think that she is guilty."

Rennert started to protest, but decided to let things stand as they were for the present.

Pérez glanced at his watch.

"I must go now to meet the doctor who returns from Mexico City. I shall bring him to the house to see the sick boy. I want very much to have the matter of his sickness settled."

"You will let me know as soon as possible what is his verdict?"

"Yes, Señor Rennert." The Captain was regarding him closely. "You seem greatly interested."

"I am. This seemingly inexplicable sickness of Esteban is now the only part of this affair that puzzles me. It may, of course, have no connection with the other events, but it is a peculiar coincidence, to say the least. When it is explained, I think that we are done with mystification."

"You understand everything, then?"

"Yes, I think I do—except for the sickness."

"*Bueno!*" Pérez smiled. "I should like to talk to you, then, when I have time." He extended a hand. "*Hasta la vista, pues, señor.*"

"*Hasta la vista, Capitán.*"

When he had gone Rennert proceeded to dress very slowly. Now that the end of the case was in sight, he felt a certain reluctance to don the executioner's hood. For that, he knew, was what it amounted to. He forced himself to think of Riddle's pale young face against the pillows. . . .

He went down to the dining room, glancing as he passed through the sala at the closed door of Madame Fournier's apartments.

Mrs. Giddings sat at the table by the window. Powder was heavy beneath her restless eyes, and her fingers moved back and forth over the cloth. A cup of coffee, black, was before her.

"Good-morning, Mrs. Giddings." Rennert approached her table.

"Good-morning! Won't you join me?" He glanced at her

THE CAT SCREAMS 163

sharply, surprised at the unusual animation in her voice. He saw now that a subtle change had taken place in her, evidenced by an eagerness that showed itself in her every action.

"How is Madame Fournier this morning?" he asked.

"All right," she said abstractedly. "She hasn't gotten up yet, but is feeling well enough, with the exception of a headache."

"I can talk to her, then?"

"Yes, but you will learn nothing. She didn't see the person who chloroformed her. She says that she went to bed and remembers only a cloth being pressed against her face."

María, the little waitress, was at Rennert's side. He smiled at her, gave his order, and asked: "You have recovered from your fright?"

She kept her eyes carefully averted.

"*Sí, señor.*" It was almost a mumble.

"You do not wish to tell me what is was that you saw?"

She cast a frightened glance out into the sala, and he thought that she was going to dart away.

"I am not sure, señor—" she spoke almost inaudibly—"I saw by the light of the candle, *nada más.* I was by the door of Esteban's room, and it was coming across the sala toward the stairs. It looked like a person, dressed in black, but the face ——" She paused and twisted her fingers together. "Out in the mountains, señor, near my pueblo, there is a cave. In it there is a figure of stone, *muy, muy antiguo.* Señor, the face that I saw last night was the face of that figure. They say that it is Tlaloc, he who brings the rains." She glanced toward the kitchen and lowered her voice still more. "You will think me very foolish, señor, but it frightened me." She moved across the tiles with quick, lithe step.

Rennert was conscious of Mrs. Giddings's scrutiny. He told her of the girl's terror the night before.

"You think she actually saw something, then?" she asked with a note of incredulity.

"Yes, although I'm not sure how much of it was her imagination. Her fright was real enough."

"You think that whatever she saw had some connection with the chloroforming of Madame Fournier?"

"Yes, and it was no incorporeal agency which pressed that towel over her face."

They sat for a moment in silence. Mrs. Giddings's fingers began to drum against the tablecloth.

"By the way," Rennert said with a laugh, "I don't believe that I thanked you last night for saving my life."

She picked up the coffee cup with unsteady fingers and drank from it.

"That was terrible, wasn't it?" She set it down. "Do you think that Miss Noon would have shot you if I hadn't come in just at that moment?"

Rennert's voice was grim: "I'm sure that she would have shot me if you had been three or four seconds later in catching her hand. I heard you in your room and hoped that you would come in before it was too late."

The muscles of her mouth and throat seemed to be suddenly tautened as she said: "Poor creature! I feel sorry for her. I wish that there were something I could do to help her."

"You did not see her again during the night?"

"No," she closed her eyes with an involuntary movement, "but I heard her—walking, walking back and forth across her room. It was terrible."

"Let us hope," Rennert said, "that she was facing the phantoms."

"Yes," she agreed slowly, "but she has horrible, horrible moments ahead of her."

"You understand, then, the meaning of that scene last night?"

"Yes, I understand it. I've had, you know, experience." Her voice trembled slightly. The morning light was cruel upon her drawn features.

"How is Esteban this morning?" Rennert asked.

Her tight lips relaxed a bit.

"Better, I believe. About daylight he had a very bad spell. I thought for a time that he was dying. The pain must have been terrible, he lay so very still. But now he's sleeping almost normally."

"You were up at daylight, then?"

"Yes," her lips adjusted themselves into a smile, "I went to my room but couldn't sleep, so I returned to his and stayed with him during the early morning hours. The hours before sunrise are the hard ones for a sick person, you know." She raised the cup again and drained it, while her eyes stared unseeingly into the mountains. "Even for Mura they were this morning," she added with another forced smile.

"For Mura?" Rennert questioned carefully.

"Yes, she acted so strangely like a frightened child when I went in to look at Madame Fournier just before daylight. She had been screaming so terribly, but when I went in she stopped and came to me and seemed to beg for affection. When I took her in my arms she clung to me as if for protection. Her little body was trembling all over. It was"—she was staring now into the empty cup as if fascinated by the grounds that remained there—"as if she sensed that something was wrong about this house."

"I hope," Rennert said, "that there will be nothing wrong about this home after today."

She looked up at him quickly.

"What do you mean?"

"The regular doctor is expected back this morning. I hope that then the quarantine will be lifted."

"Thank God!" The words came from some inner recess out of which her eyes stared moistly. "What time is he expected?" Eagerness was in her voice and upon her face as she leaned across the table.

"He ought to be here soon now. Captain Pérez has gone to meet him."

She glanced at her wrist watch.

Rennert studied her. Impatience, the frantic counting of time, was foreign to her nature as he knew it. He said: "You are ready to leave Taxco?"

"Yes," her hands were restless again, brushing against the edge of the table, "I'm ready to leave. I hoped that I might get into Mexico City in time to catch the night train for the States." She went on, speaking more rapidly: "A letter was brought to me this morning, a letter from the sanatorium that I told you about. My husband is better; they say that he has been asking for me. I must go to him."

Rennert read sudden self-consciousness in her manner as she stood up.

"You'll excuse me now," she said.

"Certainly," Rennert rose.

She turned and walked across the tiles. Her step was quick and purposeful.

When she had disappeared he stood for a moment, staring through the open doors at the opposite wall of the sala, where below the ancient musket five fiber masks had hung yesterday and where but four hung today. He was thinking: *She too has worn a mask, held on by rigid self-control. Tired muscles and nerves are rebelling now against restraint, and the mask is slipping. Therefore she appears so curiously contradictory. When the mask falls* . . . His eyes, fixed on a blank space upon the wall, narrowed, and he whistled softly to himself. Another piece of the puzzle had slid into place.

# CHAPTER TWENTY

## THE FLIGHT OF BIRDS

Esteban died just before noon that day.

The morning had become increasingly cheerless. Dark clouds hung low over the mountains, and a thin opaque haze obscured the barren slopes. Fitful winds, laden with dust, swept up through the barrancas.

From the terrace of Madame Fournier's house men could be seen upon a roof down by the plaza, hastily putting in place new bright-red tiles. In the quick step of the passers-by on the cobblestones was evident the feverish activity that possessed everyone at the long-awaited approach of the rains. Even the small flock of birds that cut in swift, unerring flight across the sky seemed moved by the same intentness of purpose.

Rennert was standing upon the terrace when Doctor Pelaez came, shortly after eleven. The doctor was a short, stout man, meticulously dressed in black. The white carnation in his buttonhole matched in whiteness his hair and mustache.

Rennert watched him stop and speak to the soldier in the street, then toil slowly up the steps and across the terrace. When he had disappeared into the sala, Rennert walked down toward the sentry. He saw the man glance upward and quickly cross himself. At the sound of Rennert's footsteps he looked around self-consciously.

"You cross yourself," Rennert said, his curiosity piqued. "You have fear of the rains?"

"No, señor," the man started to look again into the sky, but checked himself, "it is the birds."

"The birds?" Memory stirred in Rennert. "An ill omen, it is not?"

"Yes, birds that form a dark patch against the sky are a sign, they say, of illness and death. It is but another superstition of the indios, the ignorant ones, of course."

Rennert's eyes followed the flight of the birds toward the mountains.

"But the sick boy inside the house is better this morning," he said.

The Mexican shrugged, and his face had that stone-like impassivity which with his kind is too purposeful to be called stolid.

"Of course, señor," he said softly, "it is but a belief of the tontos, but I saw it—a flight of birds such as this—yesterday, just before sunset. And last night three died in Taxco, in places over which the birds flew."

"Three? There was the soldier here and the americana down at the Hotel Borda this morning. Was there another?"

"Yes, señor, there was another—another americana."

Rennert drew thoughtfully upon a cigarette.

"She killed herself," he said rather than asked.

The swift turning of the black eyes alone evidenced the soldier's surprise.

"Yes, señor. You heard?"

"I expected it, yes, but not so soon. Tell me about it."

The Mexican's gaze was lost again in contemplation of the mountainsides.

"I know but little, señor, only what I heard a little while ago. She was an old woman who has been living at the Hotel

Taxqueña. The moza found her this morning when she went to clean her room. She had killed herself during the night—with a knife. I know nothing more."

But Rennert's mind was withdrawn now from this uniformed man who stood upon the stones where the night before another such as he had died. He was thinking: *I could terrify this man and reënforce his belief in omens if I were to tell him that this is but the beginning, that before many days are past death will visit other houses over which those birds are flying. And before the despair that has been loosed upon this town his bright bayonet is helpless.*

"The gentleman who has just gone into the house," he said, "he is Dr. Pelaez?"

"*Sí, señor.*"

"And Captain Pérez did not accompany him?"

"No, he sent word that he would come at twelve, after the doctor has visited the sick boy. He is too occupied now with this matter of the americana to attend to the quarantine." The Mexican seemed abstracted, withdrawn into some inner contemplation.

Rennert turned and walked slowly up the steps. As he entered the sala the door of Esteban's room opened, and Mrs. Giddings walked out. The powder gave her tight-drawn face a ghastly aspect. She went toward the door, saying as she passed him: "Come out on the terrace, I must have some air."

They sat down in chairs, and she stared for a moment unseeingly straight ahead of her.

"Esteban," she said in a faraway voice, "is dying."

"The doctor, then, cannot aid him?"

"Not now," she said bitterly. "Had he been here earlier, or had we but known the truth, something might have been done."

"And what is the truth?"

"Acute appendicitis," she stared at her hands, which she held interlaced in her lap. "At first the symptoms are much the same as those of measles—a rash on the abdomen and on the chest; fever, muscular pains. I never saw a case of appendicitis and was influenced, I suppose, by the doctor's certainty of measles. And so we have let Esteban die. Human life should be more precious, even if it is only that of a poor little Mexican boy." Her eyes were misted by tears, staring again across the red roofs of Taxco.

Rennert said nothing. He was thinking: *Only a little Mexican boy, but upon the (to them) insignificant incident of his illness has depended the lives of these individuals penned up for two interminable days and nights under this roof and, probably, that of many others in this town. Even a little Mexican boy may have his importance in the tangled scheme of things.*

Mrs. Giddings was going on: "He is in a coma now, his appendix ruptured; in a few minutes he will be dead." Rennert sensed her unconscious perverse desire to stifle her bitterness of spirit in a flow of words. "He was a quick, intelligent boy. He used to talk to me, when I once gained his confidence, about his ambitions. He wanted to go to Mexico City and learn to paint—like Diego Rivera. He showed me some of the things that he had done, with charcoal. Who knows? He might have had talent, he might have become great, fulfilled his ambitions. Other Mexican boys have done it."

"Or," Rennert said, "he might have died in some unrecorded skirmish in these mountains, or lived out his life here in this house, telling successive guests about his unfulfilled ambitions."

She daubed at her eyes with a handkerchief and essayed a smile.

"Yes, after all, it is better to be philosophic about these things, isn't it?"

Rennert didn't look at her as he said: "Yes, even though it is cheap philosophy."

She got to her feet and thrust the handkerchief into a pocket. Her eyes were bright and eager, gazing over the mountains, northward.

"And now," she said, "the quarantine will be lifted, and I can go back—" she hesitated and added with quiet emphasis —"home."

"There only remains," Rennert said, "the matters of the murders which have been committed in this house."

"Oh!" she said with a queer catch in her voice, "I had forgotten about them."

"Perhaps," Rennert said, "that would be better."

Her eyes searched his face.

"What do you mean?"

For a moment Rennert was silent. Then he said: "The night that Shaul died you made a remark which I have remembered. You said that it was only the people without conscience who could take life easily. As I grow older I find that conscience is losing ground. It is so easy, once one learns how, to temporize with it. That is my position now—I am tempted to temporize."

"How?"

"By keeping still—attending to my own business, I might call it—I could spend a quiet vacation here in Taxco. By speaking, I would involve myself in who knows what entanglements, legal and personal. I would certainly step into the red tape of a Mexican court. I wondered what you would advise me to do." His eyes rested on her face.

"You know the truth about these deaths, then?" Her voice was toneless.

"Yes, Mrs. Giddings, I know. Whether or not the little evidence that I have would convict the guilty person is another matter. Very possibly it would not. In that case I might as well have kept still."

She straightened her shoulders and faced him.

"There is no question about what you should do," she said quietly, "and I think that in your own mind you know it."

"Yes?"

"You must speak. Duty and honor and justice are only catchwords, of course, but if we didn't have them in our vocabularies a very great deal that we set store by in our lives would fall to the ground."

Rennert nodded.

"Thank you, Mrs. Giddings."

She turned.

"You will act at once?" Her face was averted.

"Captain Pérez will be here at twelve. When he comes I shall submit my evidence to him and, if he considers it sufficient, he will arrest the criminal."

"That will be in less than an hour, then?"

"Yes, in less than an hour."

Suddenly she looked up into the sky, smiled, and said conversationally: "Look at those thunderclouds! I believe that the rains are coming at last."

Rennert thought, but could not be sure, that she was humming as she walked across the tiles.

He glanced at his watch. It marked twenty minutes until twelve. As he started to return it to his pocket his hand halted. In the sala the Siamese cat was screaming.

He realized afterwards to what extent his nerves had been tautened that morning, realized also that he had been listening more or less consciously for just that—the cries of the cat. Now that he knew the true significance of their unfailing accompaniment of death, he had come to think of them as danger signals. At the moment he was conscious only of the fact that he was standing upon the terrace, holding the watch in his hand, and that the blood was pounding erratically in his heart.

The cat stood in the doorway now, staring at him in silence. In her round blue eyes was an almost human look of agony and of appeal. Parkyn appeared in the doorway, stooped, and picked her up. She screamed again, angrily, and struggled in his arms. He turned and carried her toward the door of Madame Fournier's apartments.

When Rennert entered the sala Parkyn was closing the door. His face wore, for an instant before he looked up, a set expression of fury that made it look more than ever like that of a monarch carved upon an Assyrian wall. He rubbed the back of his left hand. "God damn that cat!" he said. "She scratched me."

He turned toward the stairs, stopped, and glanced at Rennert.

"I suppose that the quarantine is removed now that they know what is the matter with Esteban?"

"I believe," Rennert said, "that it will be soon. Captain Pérez will be here at twelve. In the meantime, guards are still posted about the house."

"Meaning that no one can leave yet?"

"Exactly that."

Parkyn patted the back of his hand with his handkerchief. "It must be almost twelve, isn't it?" he asked.

"It lacks twenty minutes." Rennert looked at the back of Parkyn's hand, thinking: *And that's another link in the chain which is growing ever tighter about this murderer!*

Parkyn said: "I'd better put some iodine on this scratch. There's always the danger of infection."

Rennert watched him ascend the stairs, then rapped at the door of Madame Fournier's quarters. There was no reply. He was about to knock again when the door of Esteban's room was opened and Dr. Pelaez emerged. As he passed Rennert on his way to the door he nodded with a preoccupied air.

"The boy is dead?" Rennert spoke softly.

The doctor paused, his black felt hat in his hands.

"Yes," he said, "he has died. There was no chance to save him, after this inexcusable delay. Had my assistant but known what the trouble was——" He shrugged, adjusted the hat on his white, carefully brushed hair, and walked out the door.

Rennert stood for a moment, staring at the scarlet noche buena flowers in the bowl by the staircase, then opened the door of Madame Fournier's apartments and knocked upon the jamb.

"*Quién es?*" Madame cried sharply from the inner room.

Rennert answered. There was a moment of silence, then: "Come in, Señor Rennert, come in!"

He walked to the beaded curtains, parted them, and opened the door to the bedroom.

Madame Fournier lay in the bed, propped up by two pillows. She looked old and tired and sick. Even her eyes had become torpid and seemed to have sunk into her face. Rennert was reminded of the eyes of a lizard, old and lethargic, lying upon a sunlit stone and staring with steady unwinking fixity at—nothing.

He stood beside the bed.

"You are feeling better, madame?"

"Yes, Señor Rennert." Weariness was in her voice.

"Mrs. Giddings tells me that you did not recognize the person who chloroformed you last night."

"No, the room was dark."

"You knew, however, that it was a woman, did you not?"

Her eyes grew a bit brighter.

"How did you know, Señor Rennert?"

"It could only have been one person. She has stood out like a flame against a drab background through this case."

Madame Fourier asked: "You know the truth, then, Señor Rennert?"

"Yes, and I should have kept still had not Shaul and Riddle died."

For a moment he stared at the woman's face, so difficult was it to see that she was still breathing.

"Let me get you something to drink, madame. It will strengthen you."

Slowly she shook her head.

"Captain Pérez will be here in a few minutes," Rennert said. "He will have the proofs of the guilt of the person who murdered those men and will make his arrest."

He went to the shelf beyond the foot of the bed and took from it a bottle of cognac and a glass. He poured some of the liquor into the glass and carried it to the bed.

"This cognac will help you," he said.

She opened her eyes and reached for the glass. She drained it and handed it back to Rennert.

"Thank you, señor."

Rennert set the glass upon the dresser and said: "I shall meet Captain Pérez in the sala, if you have no objections, madame. Most of the guests will be assembled there for lunch, and he can announce to them then that the quarantine is lifted."

"Very well, Señor Rennert, as you wish. They are all leaving, it seems, at once."

"Dr. Parkyn came to tell you that he is leaving?"

"Yes," her voice rimmed emptiness, "this house will soon be empty."

Rennert said: "*Pues, hasta luego,* madame."

"*Adiós, Señor Rennert.*"

As he closed the door he looked at his watch. It was twelve o'clock.

# CHAPTER TWENTY-ONE

Esteban's case was an extremely interesting one. Not," Dr. Parkyn amended, "from the medical viewpoint, of course. As you say, that aspect of it is simple and tragic. But it has convinced me more than ever that the Mexican Indian is a pagan at heart, despite his surface observance of Christian rituals. While the boy was delirious, all the barriers built up by contact with the white man were let down, and he was himself. A devious-minded youth who lived close to the breathing heart of nature and who, like all primitive people, feared her in most of her manifestations. The cat that screamed was a spirit threatening him."

He paced nervously back and forth in front of the door, now and then stopping to peer up at the sky. It was cloud-covered, with a curious bulging effect. Currents of air from the mountains disintegrated rapidly the wisps of smoke from his pipe.

"If he had lived, and if I had had the opportunity to study him more closely, I'm satisfied that I would have learned that some time during his life he heard of the power of some individuals to assume animal shape at will, and that he believed in it, or at least enough to fear it. Therefore, such a belief must still exist in this region. This is the nearest I've yet come to running down proof of the existence today of Nagualism. If I had more time at my disposal, I'd like to try to learn where Esteban came into contact with this belief."

Thunder rumbled in the mountains, and Rennert, standing in the dim sala, had the distinct impression that tremors passed through the floor, like vibrations from the beating of a mighty drum.

"You intend to leave Taxco soon, then?" he asked.

"Yes," Parkyn studied the bowl of his pipe, "as soon as possible. Circumstances — financial considerations — make it necessary. I had hoped to get away today, before the rains start." He glanced at his watch. "That captain ought to be here now. It's ten minutes past twelve."

Rennert watched Mandarich descend the stairs. The artist

174

was coatless and wore upon his feet plaited fiber sandals. He was yawning as he crossed the room and stood in the doorway. With the fingers of one hand he began drumming upon the wood.

"The drought's over," he announced. "You can see the rain out in the mountains. It'll be on us soon."

Parkyn walked over and joined him. Cool air brushed their faces, and they heard, still far off, the faint but persistent drumming of the rains. The sala grew darker, and Rennert walked over to the wall and switched on the electric light. Its naked effulgence gave a yellow, unnatural aspect to the room. Windows banged in the dining room, and María's sandaled feet were soft upon the tiles as she scurried past the open door.

Crenshaw came down the stairs and walked toward Rennert. He glanced toward the door where Parkyn and Mandarich stood and said in a low voice: "I understand that we're to be let out of quarantine this afternoon."

"Yes, Captain Pérez is due any minute now."

Crenshaw drew a cigar from his pocket and surveyed the end of it thoughtfully.

"You've thought about that letter I showed you — from Riddle?"

"Yes."

"Do you think it had anything to do with what has happened in this house?" Crenshaw's teeth sank into the end of the cigar as he looked at Parkyn's back.

"No," Rennert said, "I am sure now that it had nothing at all to do with what has happened."

"You think, then, that it will be all right for me to recommend Parkyn to Riddle?" Crenshaw was frowning as he lit his cigar and flipped the match to the floor.

"Yes, as far as I know, it will be all right. It might be well to ask a geologist's advice about the possibility of finding deposits of jade about here."

"Of course, I intend to do that as soon as this damned business of the quarantine is settled."

As Mrs. Giddings came down the stairs from the west wing and crossed the sala Rennert thought: *The curtain is about to go down on the last act of a play and the characters are assem-*

*bling for their final bows.* He nodded to the woman and watched her pause uncertainly by the window and stare upward at the sky. Rain drummed nearer. It could be smelled now.

"I've been wondering," Crenshaw said carefully, "if we are going to know just what lay behind these deaths before we leave?"

"Yes, you will know in a few minutes, in case you're interested."

"I am very much interested," Crenshaw said emphatically.

"Because of your desire to see justice done?"

Crenshaw said coldly: "Yes, and because a client of ours is involved. Mr. Riddle will want——"

Rain drowned the rest. It drummed upon the roof and upon the tiles of the terrace, in driving sheets that obscured vision of the outside world. Their nostrils were filled with the odor of moisture on dust.

Mandarich and Parkyn stepped back and closed the door. They stood with their backs to it and gazed about the room. A tense silence seemed to have fallen upon them all, as if voices would be futile against the pounding rain that filled the world.

"Well," Mandarich's voice boomed out, "now that we're all gathered together, somebody ought to tell us a story."

Mrs. Giddings's laugh was hysterical. She left the window and crossed to the chair that stood between Madame Fournier's door and the terrace. As she passed the bowl of scarlet noche buena flowers she pulled one out and twisted its stem between her fingers.

The door was thrown open, and Captain Pérez, shrouded in a glistening black poncho, stood between Mandarich and Parkyn. Under the drooping brim of the hat which he wore his eyes traveled quickly about the room. He closed the door. (There was a definite finality about the closing of the door, Rennert thought. It marked so unmistakably the ringing down of the curtain.)

"*Buenas tardes.*" The Mexican's eyes came to rest on Rennert's face.

"*Buenas tardes, Capitán.*"

Pérez removed his raincoat and hat and threw them across

a chair on the other side of the door. He ran a hand over his sleek black hair and said: "These people wish to know about the lifting of the quarantine, *verdad?*"

"Yes."

The Captain smiled so that his white teeth showed between his parted lips.

"The doctor has told me about the death of the sick boy, that it was all a mistake."

"A mistake, yes," Rennert agreed. *And thus summarily is Esteban dismissed,* he was thinking. *His obituary—"a mistake."*

Silence fell upon them again. Water was dripping from the poncho onto the tiles with irritating persistence.

Captain Pérez cleared his throat.

"*Amigos,*" he began, gazing about the room, "I must present to you a thousand apologies from the authorities of Taxco for your regrettable detention in this house. It was unfortunate, but—" he shrugged and polished it off with the unanswerable: "*no había remedio.* Needless to say, you are all free now to go where you wish. May I request in the name of the authorities of Taxco that you prolong your stay in our town. There are many, many places worthy of being seen—the Cathedral, of course, and the house in which lived the great scientist Humboldt. There are also——" He paused, a puzzled look upon his face, then broke into a smile and turned to Rennert. "But of course, Señor Rennert, I speak in Spanish and they do not understand. You will translate?"

Rennert did so, watching the faces about him. When he had finished there was a pause as rain beat steadily upon the tiles.

Mandarich started toward the stairs.

"Just a minute!" Crenshaw's quiet voice cut into the vacuum-like place of comparative stillness that was the room. "There is still one matter to be settled before we break up."

"Yes?" Mandarich stopped abruptly and turned to him. "What's that?"

"I think," Crenshaw said, "that Mr. Rennert can tell us." He looked for one moment into Rennert's eyes, then stared in silent absorption at the end of his cigar.

"Mr. Crenshaw is referring," Rennert said as he let his eyes travel slowly about the little group, "to the deaths of Mr. Shaul and Mr. Riddle."

The silence that held them was accentuated by the beating of the rain upon the tiles. These driving sheets of rain descending upon a parched earth gave a queer other-dimensional aspect to that bleakly illuminated room in which they stood.

Parkyn's face was hawk-like as he bent his head slightly forward in a listening attitude and squinted behind his glasses; Mandarich, stepping backward to his former position by the door, emitted a low whistle, after which his lips retained their puckered position; Crenshaw stood in front of the dining-room steps, his hands thrust in his pockets and his body swaying rhythmically back and forth as he balanced himself upon the balls of his feet; Mrs. Giddings sat very still and straight in the high-backed chair and stared at Rennert. He could see her knuckles stark white against her skin as she plucked at the scarlet flower. She pulled loose one of the petals and let it fall to the floor.

"*Qué pasa, señor?*" Captain Pérez inquired softly.

Rennert spoke to him in Spanish: "It is the matter of the murders which have been committed in this house."

"The murders?" A frown flitted across the Mexican's smooth forehead. "But what has that to do with these people? Micaela, the cook, has escaped to the mountains. There is no need to detain these countrymen of yours longer."

"Unfortunately," Rennert said, "it has a great deal to do with them. For the murderer of Shaul and Riddle is still in this house. You have received word from the articles which you sent to have tested for fingerprints?"

"Yes, a letter came this morning." He took an envelope from his pocket and extended it. He was still frowning. "The initials upon the piece of paper whose prints corresponded with those upon the light-bulb and the candle——" He paused. "There must be some mistake, señor."

Rennert opened the envelope and took out the paper.

He glanced at it, folded it again, and handed it to Pérez.

"No," he said grimly, "there is no mistake, Capitán."

"But, señor——" Pérez began. He stood facing Rennert and stared now past him.

Rennert turned and followed the direction of his gaze.

Gwendolyn Noon stood at the foot of the opposite staircase, in the outer rim of radiance from the light in the ceiling. Her face looked flushed, and her eyes, as she surveyed the little group, were bright and animated.

"Won't you join us, Miss Noon?" Rennert said.

"Are you sure I'm not intruding?" she asked with a little laugh.

"Not at all," he said. "In fact, this gathering would not be complete without your presence."

She looked at him for a moment speculatively.

"In that case," she said, "I had better join you."

With one hand she drew the cloak about her. Upon her face, as she walked unhurriedly across the sala, was a half smile of assurance, as if she knew again the delight of occupying the center of the stage. She walked past Crenshaw and sat in the chair on the other side of the door from Mrs. Giddings. She tapped a cigarette upon the back of her hand as she looked at Rennert.

"Well," she said, "proceed."

Rennert looked from one to the other of these women seated at either side of the door. Mrs. Giddings held her head high, as if in answer to a challenge, and pressed her lips tightly together. She held the noche buena flower between thumb and forefinger of one hand while with the other she jerked loose another petal. She dropped it, and a current of air swept it past her. It came to rest upon the tiles halfway between the two chairs, precisely in front of the door. It looked unpleasantly like a too-bright clot of blood. *And that,* Rennert thought, *is exactly what it is: a bright symbol of guilt.* He looked up at Captain Pérez and said: "No, Capitán, I am positive now of what I merely suspected before. The cook had nothing to do with these deaths. She took the arsenic from the kitchen and attempted to poison the cat, yes, thinking to protect Esteban. She had observed how the continued crying was preying on the boy's nerves. She may even, conceivably, have believed herself that the cat was a human being in animal shape, threatening him. She did certainly take the jade mask of Xipe from Madame Fournier's room, in the belief that it would afford some protection for one afflicted with a disease of the skin. She escaped at the first opportunity, knowing that she would be under surveillance and not wanting to run the risk of another encounter with the police. Further than this, however, she has no connection with this case. The murderer of Shaul and Riddle and your soldier, Capitán, is still in this house, is listening to me at this moment. Mr. Crenshaw here has suggested that this person be revealed before he and the rest of them leave. Have I your permission to do so?"

For an instant excitement played over the Mexican's features before they regained their immobility. His eyes were very bright and very piercing as they rested on Rennert's face.

"You are sure, Señor Rennert?"

"Yes, Capitán, I am sure."

"Very well, then," his voice was ominously controlled, "tell me who this person is."

Rennert looked at Crenshaw. The latter's eyes were fixed intently upon his face, and from a slight slow twitching of the wide nostrils and masculine mouth he fancied that, had it not been for the steady pounding of the rain, he could have heard very distinctly the man's breathing.

"Very well, Mr. Crenshaw, I have the Captain's permission to settle in your presence the matter you refer to."

By the door to the terrace there was a slight choking sound. Mandarich moved forward, his round face white and set and almost ludicrously childlike, so undisguised was its expression of alarm.

"Pardon me," he said, and sat down upon the steps that led up to the dining room. He rested an elbow upon one knee and propped his chin so that he could stare at Rennert.

Rennert raised his voice over the sound of the rain.

"All of you have been aware that something unusual has been happening in this house. Whether all of you realize that three murders—and, by implication, two others—have been committed, I don't know. At any rate, it is true. Justice has been delayed, but, to use the only available cliché, it has come at last and is about to triumph."

He paused and was aware that Captain Pérez's right hand

had stolen to his side and was resting upon the butt of his revolver.

Rennert felt somewhat like a swimmer poised for a dive as he said: "While Donald Shaul lay unconscious upstairs, two persons visited his room. One of them went, I believe, on an innocent enough errand, but upon seeing him there, helpless, yielded to an impulse and smothered him with one of the pillows on the bed. Later this person overhead a conversation in Shaul's room and realized that the pillow had been changed from the position which it had occupied and that there was a streak of blood on it. Another visit to the room, to recover the case, was necessary. Stephen Riddle, standing upon the opposite balcony, saw this person leave Shaul's room on this occasion. This person knew it and put arsenic into the bottle of cognac which stood on the young man's dresser. Considering the fact that he was evidently drinking heavily, it was almost a certainty that he would take it soon. Riddle, however, gave the cognac to Mr. Mandarich, and I got it from his room. Through carelessness for which I still blame myself, one of the sentries drank of the cognac and died."

Rennert looked at Mandarich, who had taken a handkerchief from his pocket and was passing it over his forehead.

"You were right, Mr. Mandarich. It was a narrow escape—for both of us."

Mandarich nodded dumbly.

"Another opportunity to do away with Riddle offered, however, yesterday morning, when he went to a certain room and asked for aspirin," Rennert went on. "He was given veronal instead, and doubtless advised to take a large dose. In his nervous, half-drunken condition he would not know the difference. He died, and the pillowcase from Shaul's room was put upon the floor in order to incriminate Riddle and give his death the look of suicide. The plan very nearly succeeded. It might have done so had it not been for the deaths of two American women here in Taxco."

Rennert paused and for a long moment the only sound in their ears was the drumming of the rain. It still came down with undiminished force, although by now it had assumed the rhythm of familiarity.

Rennert's eyes rested upon the scarlet petal which lay upon the floor between the chairs of Gwendolyn Noon and Mrs. Giddings. He thought of it as a target against which to direct his voice.

"The most terrible part of this whole business has been this sudden epidemic of suicides and the suffering which must have preceded them. Shaul and Riddle died painlessly. These women felt the tortures of hell before they gave up in despair in the bleak hour before dawn. One of you listening to me is suffering now, I hope, something of the anguish of facing the inevitable that these women knew. I have prolonged this speech and made it a bit melodramatic for this very purpose—to let you see retribution coming. In the arena the bull-fighter calls this, I believe, the moment of truth—when he stands over the horns." He turned and said to Captain Pérez: "And now, Captain, if you will come with me, you can make your arrest. The person whom you are going to arrest made elemental mistakes from the beginning. She forgot that her fingerprints remained upon the candle which she carried to Shaul's room. She forgot that these same prints were upon the bottle of cognac which she took from Mr. Mandarich's room, not knowing that I had substituted a marked bottle for the one which Riddle had bought and given to Mr. Mandarich. She——"

There was a rasp in Crenshaw's voice as he interrupted: "So this impersonal person you've been talking about is a woman?"

"Yes," Rennert said as he passed him, "it is a woman."

The Mexican stepped forward, his face grim and purposive, and followed Rennert toward the two women who sat on either side of the door and watched their approach.

Gwendolyn Noon was breathing heavily as she looked at Rennert over the coiling smoke of her cigarette. The hand that held the white tube trembled a bit so that ashes sprinkled her black cloak.

Mrs. Giddings sat with her head bent slightly forward and very slowly pulled the last petal from the noche buena flower. It fluttered to the floor and was carried almost to the door behind her chair.

Rain was a steady rhythm in the ears, while drippings from the tiles splashed discordantly upon the terrace.

"Mrs. Giddings," Rennert said, "when you left Shaul's room night before last, did you notice the candle which stood upon his dresser?"

She raised her head and stared at him.

"Yes," she said, "I did. It was burned down almost to the level of the bowl."

"And when you returned an hour later?"

She gasped, and the broken flower fell from her fingers.

"I remember now—there was a new one there, it had never been lighted."

Rennert nodded and stepped over the little pool of petals between the chairs and grasped the knob of the door. He shoved. Halfway, the door struck an obstacle, and he had to put his shoulder to it to force it further. He stepped into the dim anteroom and looked down at the body which lay crumpled in a grotesque heap before him.

It was the body of Madame Fournier.


## CHAPTER TWENTY-TWO

### ADIÓS

Rain lashed the laurel trees in the Plaza de Hidalgo. Rain drenched the cobblestones until they took on the appearance, in the declining afternoon light, of glistening black balloons tumbling down a torrent. The spray of rain was driven under the projecting tiles and into the little curio store where Rennert and Mrs. Giddings waited for the *camión* to Cuernavaca.

Mrs. Giddings's face looked blanched between a black tight-fitting hat and a black raincoat. She consulted her watch and said: "Only ten minutes more."

Rennert was rather worried. He looked out into the rain and said: "You won't change your mind and wait until morning, when the rains will have stopped?"

"No," her voice came very clearly through the drumming of the rain, "not if I were told that every road between here and Mexico City was likely to be washed out tonight. I've been waiting for this moment so long, holding myself under control because I knew I couldn't do Jim any good back home, that I feel like a spring that has been loosened. I must go."

Silence lay between them for a moment.

"Tell me," she said, suddenly turning to him, "about these last two days, just what happened, how you learned that Madame Fournier was the one who murdered Shaul and Riddle. I was in such a hurry to be off that I didn't hear all the details."

Rennert laughed.

"Really, Mrs. Giddings, there isn't much to tell. Madame Fournier has been conducting, for some time, I imagine, quite an extensive trade in narcotics here in Taxco. In fact, I expect that the authorities will find that she had practically a monopoly, at least among the Americans. The fact that two women, both of whom had been here for some time, committed suicide when the house was quarantined and their source of supply cut off shows that they didn't know where else to obtain them. She doubtless had a regular clientele, who came to her house for the ostensible purpose of having her consult the crystal and tell their fortunes. I remember now that when I was here before a number of Americans, particularly women, would come every day for readings. She may have been supplying them with drugs then or she may not, I don't know. My guess would be that she was just beginning her trade, since when I arrived day before yesterday I noticed obvious signs of prosperity about the house—new furniture and so forth—that had not been there last spring. I even remarked on the fact to her."

"And why did she kill Shaul? Because he knew?" Mrs. Giddings was gazing into the street, and he sensed the perfunctoriness of the question.

"Yes, he undoubtedly discovered her business and endeavored to blackmail her. His insolent manner to her when she and I were talking in the sala the afternoon I came showed rather plainly, looking back on it now, that he felt he held her under his thumb. She went to his room to take a new candle, saw him lying unconscious on the bed, and, acting on an impulse, smothered him with the pillow. It offered, you see, an excellent opportunity to do away with him with practically no danger to herself. Had it not been for her failure to turn over the pillow, no one probably would have suspected that he had not died as a result of the blow upon his head. She listened upon the balcony, however, and overheard our conversation. She understood her error and returned later to replace the pillowcases with new ones. It was when she was returning to her room that Riddle saw her from the opposite balcony."

Rennert paused to light a cigarette. He looked with narrowed eyes at the match which he held in his cupped hands.

"He was on the point of telling me of what he had seen yesterday morning when Crenshaw interrupted us." He flipped the match into the rain. "As it was, I blame myself for having given the wrong interpretation to his words. When I stood at the door of Shaul's room with Gwendolyn Noon I saw the glow of a cigarette upon the balcony opposite. When Riddle stated to me that he had been smoking there—at what time he wasn't sure—I jumped to the conclusion it was he whom I had seen. I asked him if he had seen who came out of Shaul's room. I meant, of course, Miss Noon, but didn't mention her name, since she had been the subject of our conversation. He remembered then having seen Madame Fournier walk along the balcony with the pillowcases in her hand and evidently supposed from the way I framed my question that I too had seen her. Another minute would have clarified the whole thing, but, unfortunately, Crenshaw came just then.

"Madame Fournier, meanwhile, must have been desperate. She knew that Riddle had seen her come from Shaul's room, so she was forced to get rid of him. She poisoned the cognac which stood on the table in his room. Another, and safer method of murdering him offered itself, however, when he came to her asking for aspirin. She gave him the veronal, suggesting a large dose and perhaps telling him that it was aspirin and trusting to his condition not to notice the difference, which, of course, any sober man would have done. She waited until she felt sure he had taken the veronal, then went to his room for the ostensible purpose of asking him if he wanted lunch brought to him but for the real purpose of recovering the poisoned cognac. She must have had a bad moment when

she found that the bottle was no longer in his room. While
Mandarich was at dinner she went again, for another search,
and found the bottle which I had substituted for the poisoned
one. I had marked this bottle, however, anticipating her action,
and so when I saw the marked bottle upon a shelf in her room
today I knew that I had further proof of her guilt."

As he spoke Mrs. Giddings continued to look into the rain.
She stepped forward now and peered down the street. She
glanced at her watch again.

"I thought that was the bus," she said. "It's due now." She
moved back to his side and said: "Go ahead. Don't think that
I'm not interested. It just seems somehow," she paused, "that
the arrival of this bus is so much more important now. How
did you suspect that it was Madame who was guilty and not
—say, Gwendolyn Noon?"

"It was," Rennert said, "the Siamese cat."

"The cat?" She stared at him.

"Yes, the fact that the screaming of the cat actually did
foretell death in each case. Hereafter, I'll think twice before
I laugh at an old superstition."

She continued to stare at him. He laughed.

"The explanation of the fact that the screaming of the cat
was heard before each death is simple. The cat was kept in
the anteroom of Madame Fournier's apartment, a room in
which there were no windows. Hence, the cries could be heard
throughout the house only when the door into the sala was
opened."

"Oh!" she said, and then: "Of course. That was proof, then,
that she had left her rooms."

"Yes, or at least that the door had been opened and closed.
When we heard in the dining room the screaming of the cat
and a few moments later Madame entered and told of her
discovery of Riddle's body, I was sure that this was the meaning
of the cat's cries. I was still suspicious of Gwendolyn Noon,
however, because a dope addict, suddenly deprived of his
supply, becomes unpredictable, irrational. And some of the
things that were happening—the attempt to poison the cat,
the theft of the mask of Xipe from Madame's room, for example
—didn't seem to fit. There was, too, the fact that Madame

Fournier was afraid of someone in the house. She wouldn't open her door until I identified myself. I linked the bruise upon Gwendolyn Noon's elbow with the broken crystal and her visit to Madame and decided that she had struggled with the old woman. There could be only one explanation for this visit—her desire to obtain drugs. Madame had overpowered her but was afraid of another visit. Madame was doubtless superstitious enough to put some credence in the belief that a broken crystal is a bad omen and connected this with another visit from Miss Noon. At first I couldn't account for the missing blotting paper from the pad in Shaul's room until I connected it too with the drug traffic. When she feared detection Madame had doubtless resorted to an old device and given her customers blotting papers saturated with morphine or cocaine. They could carry these from her house without arousing suspicion. Gwendolyn Noon knew this and, in her desperation, seized upon every piece of blotting paper which she saw in the hope that it might possibly contain the drug which she was seeking. It was morphine, I am sure. Morphine in the form of crystals or powder is easily soluble in water. When Captain Pérez and I interviewed her in my room and I asked her to look at the piece of paper, I noticed her interest in the blotting paper in the drawer of my table. Later, when I found that my room had been entered and the blotting paper taken from it, I knew that Miss Noon entered the picture as the drug addict but not as the slayer of Shaul. Because, if Shaul had been dispensing drugs and she had murdered him, she would have gotten a supply from his room. The problem was half solved then.

"I went over the available list of suspects for the dope dispenser and selected Madame Fournier as the most logical. There was a reference in one of Donald Shaul's columns which I read on the train coming down here to Gwendolyn Noon's dabbling in crystal-gazing. This, combined with her statement that he had learned enough about her to know of her previous marriage, was a pointer to Madame. When I asked her if she had ever suspected Shaul of selling drugs (at first, I was inclined to believe that this had been the reason for his murder) she grew wary and tried to throw suspicion upon him, saying

that he always had much money. During the same conversation
her curiosity about Riddle struck me as more than casual.
When I heard of the suicide of the first of the American
women I was convinced that it was Madame who was the drug
seller. I remembered, you see, having seen an American woman
trying to get past the sentry the morning after the quarantine
was declared. She told him that she wanted to come to Madame
for a reading of the crystal. When Dr. Otero's instrument
case disappeared I felt sure that Gwendolyn Noon had taken
it in the hope of finding drugs in it. This meant, of course,
that she was still unable to obtain a supply. The sight of the
chloroform doubtless gave her the idea of making Madame
Fournier unconscious while she searched her rooms. She did
so and found a supply of the drug-saturated blotting paper.
But upon starting across the sala she saw María coming from
the door of Esteban's room. You and I were upon the terrace,
so escape was cut off in that direction. She acted quickly, took
one of the masks from the wall, and held it over her face while
she walked to the stairs. María, of course, was terrified by the
sight and fainted. When I saw the blotting paper in Miss
Noon's room I knew beyond the shadow of a doubt that
Madame Fournier was selling drugs. This, then, gave a motive
for her removal of Shaul—self-protection. The pinning of the
murders upon her was easy then."

"But what proof did you have—beyond the screaming of the
cat?" Mrs. Giddings asked, taking her gaze for an instant
from the street.

Rennert was thoughtful for a moment.

"As a matter of fact," he admitted, "I doubt whether she
could have been convicted upon the evidence which I had.
There was really, you see, nothing but her fingerprints upon
the candle which she had carried to Shaul's room and upon
the light-bulb in my room. The wax which had melted and
run down the sides of the candle of course bore Miss Noon's
fingerprints, for it had fallen, and she had righted it while I
was in the room with her. When that wax had cooled, however, I removed it, and the fingerprint expert in Cuernavaca
found Madame's underneath it. The candle itself, regardless
of the prints, constituted fairly good proof that she had gone

to Shaul's room. I heard him tell her that he needed a new candle, and when I went there at nine-thirty a new candle was upon his dresser. And, as I heard Madame repeat again and again, she was forced to do all the work of caring for the rooms while Esteban was sick. This, however, would prove nothing beyond the fact that she had gone to the room, contrary to her own statement. Nevertheless, I sent the candle, the light-bulb, and a specimen of the fingerprints of Madame, Gwendolyn Noon, and Dr. Parkyn for examination. I obtained specimens of the prints of the last two when Captain Pérez and I interviewed them, and I already had one of Madame's upon a piece of notepaper which she had used as a bookmark in your copy of Tennyson. The fresh scratches upon the back of Riddle's hand had clearly been made by a cat, which fact constituted proof that he had been in her room but not necessarily that he had gotten the veronal from her. I hoped to pull the old game of bluffing into a confession a suspect against whom one does not have sufficient evidence to convict, so I took care to let her know that the murderer would be revealed at noon, when Captain Pérez came, and counted on the fact that she would be listening behind the door of her room. I prolonged my speech so as to drive home to her my conviction of her guilt. She took poison—the last of the arsenic—and was dead when I opened the door."

The camion was an antediluvian beast lumbering through the rain. It came to a stop, as if settling wearily, at the corner of the plaza, and a raincoat-sheeted figure jumped off. His voice was shrill through the rain: "Taxco!" An Indian woman, covered by a shawl and carrying a large basket, stepped down with difficulty and waded through the torrent. She slipped upon the cobblestones, and from the tilted basket a bunch of white calla lilies fell. They lay for a moment, held by the stones, while their whiteness stared forth from the swirling muddy stream. Water dislodged them then, and they were carried down the hillside, a momentary mud-covered dam in the current.

Mrs. Giddings stared at them and said through lips that scarcely moved: "Like the beauty that artists see in Taxco, sullied by reality." She turned and picked up a suitcase from the floor.

Rennert was silent as he took the other suitcase and a hatbox and followed her toward the street.

"And yet," he said, "it is the rain that renews Taxco's flowers."

Rain drenched them now. He followed her across the slippery stones and assisted her to climb up the steps. He handed the luggage to the impatient driver and turned to her. She was standing upon the top step, shaking the water from her raincoat.

"You're going to wait for the new flowers, then?" she asked in a voice that held a laugh.

"Yes," he smiled, "they always appear, sooner or later. *Adiós.*"

The driver stepped between them and climbed the steps.

"*Adiós,*" she called past him.

Rennert crossed the stones to the shelter of the arcade. He stood there and watched the car disappear into the rain on the twisted street that leads to the mountains.

THE END

CPSIA information can be obtained
at www.ICGtesting.com
Printed in the USA
BVHW030920060222
628175BV00001B/18